Art of Being a Billionaire

Three billionaire brokers...three chances at forever?

A charismatic trio of brokers have built a billion-dollar
empire buying, selling and discovering new artworks.
Their dashing good looks and smooth-talking charm
have even earned them a TV show and their own
on-screen personalities: Krew is The Brain, a sharp
intellect and a wiz at auction. Joss is The Brawn,
a gorgeous thrill seeker with muscles to match.
And Asher is The Face, a handsome devil who can
charm his way into any art deal.

But in the high-stakes art world, where everything
could be lost in an instant, are any of them
willing to risk it all for love?

Find out what happens when Asher Dane's plan to
take on a coveted new client leads him
to a relationship retreat in Iceland with
captivating receptionist Maeve Pemberton
posing as his girlfriend in

Faking It with the Boss
Available now

Will The Brain and The Brawn also get their shot
at finding true love?

Find out in Krew's and Joss's stories,
coming soon!

Dear Reader,

This story begins a three-book series, Art of Being a Billionaire, that focuses on three college friends who formed an art brokerage to share their love of art. Of course, they have a TV series that, during the opening credits, labels them: The Brain, The Brawn and The Face. Let's start with The Face, aka Asher Dane, and his story. He was interesting to me because he's gotten through a rough time in life by putting on a mask that attracts and charms with ease. But that's not really him. Of course not. It can never be that easy.

When I write a story, I always include bits from my life. It could be a favorite painting, a part of my personality that echoes out from the heroine, a love for a specific type of hero (Tall, dark and handsome? Yes, I'm a cliché.). Or even a desire to visit a fantasy-like location, such as the Blue Lagoon in Iceland, that I will get to someday.

Enjoy!

Michele

FAKING IT WITH THE BOSS

MICHELE RENAE

ROMANCE

Harlequin®
ROMANCE

ISBN-13: 978-1-335-21630-4

Faking It with the Boss

Copyright © 2025 by Michele Hauf

Harlequin Enterprises ULC
22 Adelaide St. West, 41st Floor
Toronto, Ontario M5H 4E3, Canada
www.Harlequin.com

Printed in U.S.A.

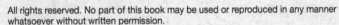

Michele Renae is the pseudonym for award-winning author Michele Hauf. She has published over ninety novels in historical, paranormal, and contemporary romance and fantasy, as well as written action/adventure as Alex Archer. Instead of "writing what she knows," she prefers to write "what she would love to know and do" (and yes, that includes being a jewel thief and/or a brain surgeon).

You can email Michele at toastfaery@gmail.com.
Instagram: @MicheleHauf
Pinterest: @ToastFaery

Books by Michele Renae

Harlequin Romance

A White Christmas in Whistler

Their Midnight Mistletoe Kiss

If the Fairy Tale Fits...

Cinderella's Billion-Dollar Invitation

Cinderella's Second Chance in Paris
The CEO and the Single Dad
Parisian Escape with the Billionaire
Consequence of Their Parisian Night
Two Week Temptation in Paradise

Visit the Author Profile page at Harlequin.com.

For Mary and Lois. We basically rock.

Praise for
Michele Renae

"Renae's debut Harlequin [Romance] novel is a later-in-life romance that's sure to tug at readers' heartstrings."

CHAPTER ONE

ASHER DANE STROLLED into The Art Guys' London office, inhaling the subtle scent that always calmed him yet at the same time seemed to sharpen his senses. Lemon. It was the receptionist's doing. A tiny terra-cotta scent pot sat on the corner of her desk. She—Maeve—commandeered front and center of the circular office space, with three private offices and the large meeting room curving along the back. The curvaceous area enhanced the appeal of their product, which was art.

Even more so, the receptionist gave good curb appeal as she looked up, nodded, then spoke to whoever it was on her headset. That tiny smile of hers, barely there, always managed to capture his attention. Because at the corners of her mouth were perfect little apostrophes. They enticed him. Made him want to trace them. With his lips.

Asher caught himself before he walked into a Grecian amphora displayed on a pedestal. A five-hundred-thousand-pound deduction from his paycheck should the vase shatter. He swerved, but his gaze snatched one more glance. That intriguing grin. It said there was more to the woman than met the eye.

And yet, he rarely spoke to her save for long-distance office calls. Not because he didn't have an interest in learning more about the petite dark-haired woman who had worked for them for two years. She'd been hired six months after he'd rejoined Krew and Joss here as a permanent broker. Rather, those almost-smiles she cast him made him believe she wasn't interested or impressed by him. Perhaps even judging him for things he'd rather not think about but tended to consider at odd times, like when he was brushing his teeth or sitting with a paddle in hand waiting for an art auction to begin.

For heaven's sake, he didn't know what to do when in the same room as her. Not a feeling he was accustomed to. And that annoyed him.

"Ash!" Joss Beckett poked his head out of Krew's office and waved him inside. "Excellent timing. Get in here!"

Passing by Maeve's desk, Asher slowed, and she glanced up at him with glittery green eyes surrounded by the lushest black lashes. He winked at her. Her mouth, deliciously dark cherry and curvy, dropped open. Whoever was on the other end of the line prompted her to a flustered apology.

Wrong move, man! He'd spoiled her concentration.

Asher darted into the office. Why did he assume idiot mode around that woman?

"Good to see you, Asher. Have a seat."

Krew Lawrence leaned back in his chair, feet up on the desk. A tidy tweed vest worn over white shirtsleeves rolled to his elbows was his usual garb. His nickname for the show? The Brain. Fitting. Asher had met him at university, and they had bonded over their love of art. Krew handled the legal and accounting for the trio's billion-dollar empire.

Over the last decade, the university friends had come together through their love for all manner of art and formed a brokerage. They bought, sold, discovered and appraised, and had acquired an A-list of celebrity clients and accomplished artists. Halfway through that decade though, Asher had been forced to leave the trio to care for his ailing parents. But after finally finding them the proper care, Asher had been able to return to the team almost three years ago. It had been right before Krew and Joss had been approached by a major television network to do a short-run series. Last month, they'd wrapped filming on their second season. Six episodes that followed their quests for rare artwork, the travails of high-stakes auctions, and even that one episode that had featured him and Joss helping a ninety-year-old woman go through a Highgate apartment that had been locked and preserved since before World War II—that had netted millions in rare and previously unknown artwork.

Asher loved being in front of the camera. When others were watching he was at his best. The way to garner attention was to flash his pearly whites and give them what they expected: a surface glamour that no one cared to see beneath. They hadn't nicknamed him The Face for the show for nothing. The label didn't bother him. He'd always been called handsome, and hell, he knew how to use his looks to get what he wanted. Yet sometimes he got so focused on the outer glamour and what it could get for him that he wasn't even sure anymore who Asher Dane was.

He veered his attention back toward reception. Apparently, no matter how much he utilized his patented charm, some things were unattainable. Such as Maeve's interest. How she frustrated him! And those bold colors and mismatched prints she always wore. There were days it hurt his eyes to even glance in her general direction.

"We have a job for you, Asher." Krew, ever on a schedule and always the first to spot a forgery, wasn't one for hellos or pleasantries.

"I've been on the road two months, and the first time you see me, you shove another job in my face?" Asher teased. Then he laughed, meeting Joss with playful punches to one another's shoulders. "How you doing, man? Did the trip to Brazil take it out of you?"

"Almost got squeezed to death by a giant python," Joss said, nicknamed The Brawn for the show for good reason. The man had the muscles and the fearless audacity to rush headlong into adventure, be it a scuba diving mission to search for a lost ancient sculpture or tackling a swarm of bees that had overtaken a castle's art room. "You look good. But then, you always do."

"It's a curse." Asher sat on the velvet chair before Krew's desk. Everything in the office was curved and no hard lines. The decor had been Asher's doing. He loved the romantic aesthetic. Yes, he was a sucker for the Pre-Raphaelite period. Modern, blocky, light-starved Mondrian and Picasso? He'd leave the geometric stuff to Krew. "What's up with this new job? And don't I have a thing in Bangladesh soon?"

"You do. But I think you can squeeze this one in." Krew turned his laptop around.

The screen displayed an article about Tony Kichu, "relationship coach to the stars." Asher skimmed the text, which detailed the eccentric man's methods of coaching via Zoom. None of his clients had ever met him in person, though he was a billionaire due to his cultlike following.

"Apparently," Krew said, "the man is also an artist. His clients want to buy his work but he won't sell."

"What's his style? His medium?" Asher scrolled the page but there wasn't any mention of Kichu's art.

"No one knows beyond that he paints."

Asher diverted his attention between both men's gazes. Each was thinking the same thing. "Then how does anyone know they want it?"

"Because of his fame," Joss said. "Isn't that how it always goes?"

"Fair enough. So what?" Asher leaned back in the chair. "You want me to talk to the guy?"

"Yes, and get a look at his work. If we can snag him as an artist…"

"We could use another buzzworthy artist to introduce to the world," Krew said.

"Buzz is always good," Joss added. "And…" He sighed.

Yes, yes, the unspoken rang loudly in Asher's head. He'd yet to bring in his own artist. Sure, he handled a list of elite clients, and he could buy and sell at auction like no one's business. But he'd been out of the business those years he'd been taking care of his parents, and when he had been here at the beginning his focus had been garnering publicity and making a name for the trio.

But now? Whether the guys ever said it out loud—and he knew they never would—bringing in an artist would finally prove Asher's true worth to them. That he was the entire package. That he contributed as much talent and skill as his two colleagues.

A gruff voice from his recent past muttered in his thoughts.

You're subpar, Dane. There's no substance behind the pretty face.

A comment that had gutted Asher not once but over and over, as it had been recorded and shown on the TV series.

It wasn't true. He wasn't subpar. He could hold his own alongside Krew and Joss, but... He hadn't a stable of artists to nurture and hone and bring to the world to show that The Art Guys really was the number one brokerage with the most unique and talented artists.

"And," Joss added, "nabbing Tony Kichu would be another notch for your social media."

"It's not a notch, Joss. Just another post and tons more followers for *our* socials."

Asher spent time enhancing his online presence and that of the brokerage. He had over five million followers. That kept The Art Guys in the news. He was providing value to the team in that manner.

But to finally bring in an artist? That was paramount.

"I can do it," Asher said. "Where's the guy at? And if he doesn't meet personally with his clients… I really hate to do an appraisal via Zoom."

"You won't have to. Kichu holds a couples' spa retreat once a year at his home base just out of Reykjavík."

"Iceland? Nice place to visit this time of year. And a spa? Swing in. Soak in the geothermal pools. Then finagle a meeting with Kichu. No problem."

"There is one problem." Krew turned the laptop back around and stood. "It's a couples' retreat so you'll need a significant other on your arm. You dating anyone at the moment?"

"That's a stupid question," Joss said. "The Face always has a woman on his arm."

True. Dating beautiful women made for good content on his socials. Though it never seemed to fill his emotional content bucket. Currently, Asher was between women.

Honestly? The surface-level connections he made were not cutting it anymore. He craved real connection, and something that lasted longer than a weekend. At thirty-two, he wasn't getting any younger, and much as he'd never admit it to his proudly single business mates, he did want to start a family.

"Totally single right now."

Both his coworkers stared at him in disbelief.

Asher shrugged. "What can I say? Sometimes even The Face needs a break."

"Well, you need to get a woman. Fast," Krew said. "I've already had our Maeve book a flight and tickets for the retreat. Plane leaves tomorrow evening and the retreat begins the next day."

He expected nothing less than last-minute orders from Krew. "Well…" Asher rubbed his jaw.

He did have a few regulars he tended to hook up with, but the idea of spending a week with someone he wasn't close to? Iffy. And while he had a type—sexy, smart, independent, usually had their own influencing gig—none had ever felt like go-the-distance girlfriend material. Like someone with whom he could share a future.

That shouldn't matter if he intended to fake being in a couple.

"Why not bring along our Maeve?" Joss suggested.

The other two men cast their gazes toward reception.

Asher smirked. "You guys do know that calling her *our Maeve* makes her sound like some kind of Jane Austin character?"

"I rather like Jane Austin," a female voice said.

Asher turned as Maeve entered the office and set a bulky folder on Krew's desk. She wore a slim-fitted Maxfield Parrish blue dress that emphasized her long legs and tiny waist. It had a wide green paisley collar and matching turned-back cuffs at the short sleeves. Some kind of retro look, he decided. It suited her. Even if the paisley clashed wildly with the striped blue fabric. But those severe black bangs. Another retro style, perhaps. He preferred his women with long lush locks and silk shirts beneath a business suit.

Yet, oh, those apostrophes hugging her lips. And the way the afternoon light beamed across her pale skin...

"Did I hear my name?" she asked.

"She's *our* Maeve," Krew said, smiling at her, "because we love her. And Maeve is family."

"Family?" Asher looked to the receptionist to see how she would react to that overly familiar label.

"I like it when Krew calls me our Maeve," she offered succinctly. "He's like my smart big brother who watches out for me. And when Joss says it, it's also nice. He's my little brother who would fight a guy to protect me."

"Damn right I would," Joss agreed.

Really? They were a family? When and why had *he* been left out of this secret office alliance? Sure, he traveled a good ninety percent of the working calendar, but he stopped in at least once a month for in-person meetings.

"Maeve, would you like to accompany Asher on the spa trip?" Krew asked. "As you booked the reservations, you are aware it is a couples' retreat. Asher doesn't have a partner to go along with him, so if you'd like to...?"

Asher sat upright. The guys were rushing ahead with a plan they hadn't discussed with him! And sure, he wouldn't mind a little get-to-know-you time with *our Maeve*, but he didn't want them to push her into it. Or him. Because there was that issue of not knowing how to breathe around her or act, or talk, or—

"You need me to..." She paused, glancing briefly to Asher. Was that panic on her face? "Fake being Mr. Dane's partner?"

"It's just for show," Krew said. "It would look a bit odd if he showed up alone."

"A week holiday at a spa?" she asked. "Paid for by the company?"

"All expenses," Krew reassured. "You've been wanting us to consider you for fieldwork. This might be a good chance to watch Asher in action, get some tips and see how you can assist. He can assess your talent and give us feedback."

Assess her talent? Oh, he'd assessed her. Plenty of times. And—what was going on?

Maeve nodded eagerly, but when she again

glanced to him, her smile fell. Gone were those enticing punctuation marks. "Is that all right with you, Mr. Dane?"

Why did she call them Krew and Joss while he was always Mr. Dane? What had he done to alienate the one person in this office who seemed to fascinate and confuse him at the same time?

"It'll work," he offered. He was used to putting on a show, charming the clients, saying whatever was needed to win the deal. Over the years, it had grown much easier to be The Face than Asher Dane.

"Can you be ready to leave by tomorrow evening?" Krew asked Maeve.

"Of course! That'll give me most of the day to take care of any office work that needs attention over the next week."

Even as she spoke she strolled around Krew's office, tugging open a cabinet drawer and pulling out a big file. That slim-fitted skirt hugged her slight curves and… Assess her? Oh, he was up for that job.

"Joss is due in Las Vegas next Tuesday," she said. "And you, Krew, have the DeSevre's auction in town. I'll make sure everything is prepared. And if you need me you can always call." She left, breezing toward her desk, answering a call on her headset even as she sat.

Asher turned to face his friends. Both wore cat-snuffling-cream smirks on their faces. "What?"

"We know," Joss said conspiratorially.

Krew wore one of those sneaky smiles that indicated *I know things you think I don't.*

"You don't know," Asher defended. But what it was they thought they knew, he wasn't even sure about.

"Oh, we know," Krew said. He met Joss with a fist bump. "We know."

Asher spun on the chair to spy Maeve sorting through a file folder while simultaneously speaking with a client. Her long legs were crossed gracefully and her body tilted forward. She wore the Parrish blue dress like the artist himself had mixed the vivacious color especially for her.

He was to spend the next week with her at a couples-only private spa?

Maybe they *did* know.

CHAPTER TWO

MAEVE MET HER FLATMATE, Lucy, at the front door of their two-bedroom flat in Fulham. The West London neighborhood had been an ideal landing spot for Maeve when she'd moved there from Dublin five years earlier after landing her first job with a local art gallery. The neighborhood was filled with colorful Victorian houses and pubs, and the food shops offered delicious cuisine. And it was a short walk to nearby Bishops Park, where she liked to linger in the rose garden on weekends.

Lucy had parlayed her gregarious and slightly theatrical charm into a cushy job as a makeup influencer, so she was always home. In her bedroom, sitting beneath perfect lighting, doing her thing. Maeve could tell that she was looking forward to having the place to herself while she was away because it would allow her to pack. Lucy was getting married next month, which would leave Maeve in need of a flatmate to cover the rent that sucked up a third of her income.

Maeve had met Lucy the day she'd arrived in London. She had been sulking in a coffee shop because the idea of staying with her dad in his open studio, along with his snooty girlfriend, had given her a gut ache. She and Lucy shared a common love for natural history nonfiction, sugary breakfast pastries and weird decorating aesthetics. Lucy had encouraged Maeve to go wild when decorating the apartment and they both agreed the flat looked like "Martha Stewart meets Cottagecore meets Alice in Freakin' Wonderland." Color was Maeve's means of expressing herself.

Another instant bond had been their shared dreams of owning a shop. Maeve had been the idea woman; Lucy was the accounting, marketing and all-that-financial-stuff woman. They'd opened their shop almost a year to the day after that auspicious meeting over coffees. Calling it Fuchsia, the shop had sold color in every form, from kitschy home decorations, to paints and markers. Colored papers and fabrics. Anything to add color to a person's life. Maeve's ultimate dream was to eventually parlay the shop into a consulting business in which she would help people design rooms or entire households through color.

It had been lovely, exciting, and…one month after the official opening the pandemic had hit.

They'd had to close two months later. Their inventory had been sold to pay lenders—namely, Maeve's mother—but Maeve's dream to own a shop, this time specifically related to color consultation, still shone brightly in her heart.

Maeve had admired how Lucy had pivoted like a pro. She was a marvel with makeup, and even did occasional "look-alike" posts where she transformed her face into that of a celebrity. Her Adele look was spot-on. Her fiancé was a world traveler, so she intended to wave goodbye to London and head out on an adventure.

Lucy nudged Maeve's hardshell suitcase, purple with white skull polka dots. "Are you sure you can do this, sweetie?"

So much in that simple question. Maeve knew that Lucy was aware of her desire to reopen her business. And that she needed to increase her earnings to do so. And that she would never again ask her mum for a loan. Mariane Pemberton's oft-repeated epitaph for her daughter was "you've failed."

Recently named one of the top fifty investors under fifty, Maeve's mother was a go-getter multimillionaire who had built her own investing firm geared toward women. If a person wasn't working or thinking about work, or moving up the corporate ladder, they had failed at the game of life. Which was why Maeve's dad had divorced his wife eight years ago. Maeve was much more her father's daughter when it came to tackling life as it was thrown at her. Of course, her father was currently a kept man—his girlfriend had a trust fund—so that's where the comparison stopped.

Maeve grabbed the handle of her suitcase. "Of course, I can luxuriate in a spa for the next week with no cares but to look at some art, Lucy!"

"Those hot springs are supposed to be the fountain of youth. Not that you need it, you and your porcelain skin. Lord, I wish I had cheekbones like yours." Lucy fluttered her fingers over her face. "I wouldn't have to contour!"

"You don't need to," Maeve said. "You are beautiful with or without makeup."

Lucy gasped. "No one will ever see this face without the war paint."

"I have."

"And you will take that knowledge to your grave." Lucy touched Maeve's bangs, adjusting them. Maeve ruled the decorating; Lucy had free rein over all hair and makeup decisions. "I know you'll enjoy the vacation part of the adventure, but you *know* what I'm really asking you."

Maeve sighed heavily. Never in a million years would she have thought one of her fantasies would come true. And to be literally thrust into a quasi-relationship with the one man she lusted over?

"He's my boss. He needs a fake girlfriend. I need the points with my other two bosses if I'm to move up in the company. My dream to reopen the shop as a consulting business will never happen unless I increase my finances."

"It'll happen. You have a gift, girl. You need to spread the color around. But seriously. You slyly bypassed the fact that you have crushed on The Face since day one."

"The whole world crushes on Asher Dane. There's nothing special about that. He's handsome. He's also…a little cold, I'd say. He rarely speaks to me unless it's directly related to the business." She made to step around Lucy. Asher had texted he'd pick her up for the airport in ten minutes.

Lucy sidestepped to block access to the doorknob—clear crystal set against a lavender-painted wood door with pale pink stripes.

"Yes," Lucy said, "but the whole world does not dream about staring at artwork with Mr. Dane. Just…lolling there. Looking at it. I don't get it," she said of the oft-visited fantasy Maeve had once divulged. She shook her head and gestured dismissively. "I'll never understand you art people."

"Says the woman who literally creates art on her face."

"So true."

"As for my fantasy… Mr. Dane sees things in art," Maeve said. She'd watched Asher lose himself in a painting. Often. It was remarkable to behold. It was exactly as she did when she viewed a beautiful piece of art. She fell into the story of it. "Don't worry. You know Mr. Dane never gives me the time of day. This week at the spa is pretend."

"You pretending to be his girlfriend? I know exactly where that's headed." Lucy winked. "If you're lucky."

"Please, Lucy. It's not going to be like one of those silly romance movies we like to watch over popcorn and beer."

"Yeah? Sweetie, you know those stories always end with the girl getting the guy."

Maeve sighed. If only the same could happen to her. But she was a realist. And Asher was not the sort of man who would date a girl like her. He dated models and celebrities. She was weird and color-crazy Maeve, a displaced expat from Dublin who had dreams of owning her own business.

Of finally proving to her mum that she could be a success.

"I already know the ending," she said to Lucy.

"And the credits are not going to roll *happily ever after*. Besides, I'll be on the clock. I need to study Mr. Dane's style to see how he gets the job done if I'm ever to impress the other bosses."

"Oh, we both know you've studied his *style* far too much already."

"Lucy!"

Her friend narrowed her gaze at her, capped by perfectly sculpted brows, and leveled her with a firm, "Maeve."

Lucy was right. As well as being incredibly alluring regarding his passion for art, the man was not terrible to look at. Maeve crushed on him. Hard. And so maybe she had plans to enjoy this week of pretending she was in a relationship with him. Why not? It would be the closest she ever got to the fantasy. But she'd be careful not to let her heart into the deal. Her mum always said love complicated things. It's why she and Maeve's dad couldn't make it work. Mariane Pemberton had chosen success over love.

"Something good will come of this," Lucy said with a glint in her eye.

"Me being promoted?"

Lucy tilted her head, assessing. "Maybe."

"I don't know what else could come of it." Yes, she could dare to dream that Asher Dane would fall madly in love with her, drop to his knees and propose to her.

"Exactly," Lucy decided, as if reading Maeve's wildly fantasizing thoughts.

Keep it fantasy, she warned inwardly. *Business not pleasure.*

Checking her texts, Maeve opened the door and fled, calling back, "I'll see you in a week!"

Lucy's call echoed down the hallway, "At the very least, get a kiss out of the deal!"

Rolling her eyes as she entered the lift, Maeve pressed the button for the main floor and clutched her suitcase handle. She had no intention of crossing any work boundaries, especially when she wanted to prove herself to Krew and Joss. This week must be nothing more than a relaxing—and learning—vacation.

Once out of elevator, she stepped outside into the warm July air as a limo pulled up. The back window rolled down and Asher Dane winked at her.

Maeve's stomach flip-flopped like a giddy guppy. Her cheeks flushed as well. Mercy, this was not going to be a relaxing vacation if the man released one more of those electrifying winks on her.

Keep it together. It's just pretend.

And she had best keep her fantasies to herself.

The three-hour flight allowed them to do a bit of homework on one another. Over wine provided by first class, they shared highlights of their university info. He'd attended the Royal College of Art and had majors in art history and social sciences. Maeve had taken a year of art from Westminster, with a side of business management thrown in.

Asher's suspicion Maeve had grown up in Ireland was confirmed. Her accent was faint. Her father was British but her mother was Irish. Both parents had initially traveled for their jobs. After her parents divorced and her mum had permanently relocated to New York, Maeve had moved to London to try her feet in the business world and she'd lived there since.

Asher had lived in London all his life. He'd always strove to stay close to his parents. He hadn't explained to Maeve about his parents' conditions. It wasn't necessary for their one-week fake relationship. And no one wanted to hear the real-life stuff that tended to throw a wrench into the fantasy of reality. Besides, having retired to a quiet country home in Bath, Mr. and Mrs. Dane were doing well so long as they stayed off the grid.

"So you and Krew and Joss met at uni?"

She had turned on the seat and tucked up her legs to face him. Her petite frame was all black hair and peach linen. It would easily be possible to fit two of her in the seat. She'd slipped off her

strappy green heels to reveal tiny violet toenails.
Yet it was her lipstick that drew his gaze. Deep
red, almost like velvet, with tones of blood-dark
crimson. And those two tiny apostrophes that always gave the appearance of a smile even though
her eyes often said otherwise. He wondered what
her mouth might taste like…

"Mr. Dane?"

She had caught him looking. When he noticed
the stern glint in her eyes, he shook himself from
his foray into a kiss and composed himself.

"You should stop calling me Mr. Dane if we're
to appear as a real couple."

"Good call. Asher." With a lift of her chin, she
asked, "And do you remember *my* name?"

"What? Of course."

"Really? Last week you called me Marsha.
And I've heard you mutter Minnie, Morgan and
even Alice as you march past my desk to your
office."

"I do not march. I never *march*," he insisted.
More like a careful stroll, ever cautious he might
trip or do something ridiculous to completely hu-
miliate himself before the remarkable and mysterious Maeve.

There was something about using a person's
real name that weirdly flustered him. It was intimate. Most of the time, with men, he used their
surnames. And women he could easily name

darling or babe, or some nonsense. But naming *her* felt intense. Like he was claiming her. Making her his own.

You have to play along for this fake-a-week adventure.

"Minnie is a nice name," he said. "So is Margot, Morgan and Estelle."

She gave him that disapproving smirk he was so accustomed to receiving from her. Admittedly, he did like to tease. Get a reaction. It was how he gauged people's interest. It was a tool he utilized to move through life.

Her mouth compressed, which curled those apostrophes even more.

"Maeve," he stated. He liked the feel of her name in his mouth. Short, simple, but like delicate artwork that required study. "Very close to *mauve*, which is about the best color ever. And don't get me started on its invention in the nineteenth century."

"William Perkin, a chemistry student was synthesizing quinine from coal tar for a malaria treatment when he happened upon the mauve dye."

Asher snapped a look at her. How did she...?
"Right, an art student. A lifelong love?"

"Since I used to scribble with coloring crayons and markers. Still do, actually. An intense love for color lives in me. Mauve, carmine and emerald run through my veins."

God, he loved that statement. And to imagine? Such a lush manner of speaking about one's passion. Truly, why had he never dared to converse with *our Maeve* before?

"One day I will own a Maxfield Parrish lithograph," she stated proudly.

"Love the saturated colors that man utilized. Such whimsy. And the curves."

"Your artistic preferences do tend toward the curvy."

Asher crooked a brow, but she didn't notice his curiosity as she handed her empty wine goblet to the passing flight attendant. How did she know what he preferred? He was rarely in the office.

"So how long have we been dating?" Big green eyes peered at him from beneath lush black lashes. "It'll be helpful to know what the intimacy level should be. If we don't want to send up any red flags, we'll have to act as if we've known each other awhile."

"A year?"

"Oh." She tugged in her lip with her teeth, and the action drew his attention intensely. Those perfect white teeth. Yet, she was worried?

"Too long?" he wondered.

"That would imply we know each other quite well and might have to…"

Was she afraid they might have to hold hands or kiss? Best way to convince others they were a couple. Did she have anything against kissing him? He supposed it was a lot to ask of an employee. Perhaps she worried about employer/employee fraternization?

"A few months," he tossed out. "Long enough to know a little about one another and to have googly eyes for each other, but not so long that we've, you know."

"Yes, I know."

Did everyone know? Apparently, they did. Thinking back to Joss and Krew stating as much in the office, Asher had to laugh. And before he could answer Maeve's question about why he was laughing, the pilot announced their landing.

He clasped her hand and gave it a squeeze. "Ready?"

A genuine smile beamed in her eyes, and it grabbed him by the heart and squeezed. Quite unexpected. What was it about the deliciously intriguing yet weirdly colorful Maeve Pemberton?

"Not completely ready," she said with a brave inhale, "but let's do this anyway."

"Less sure than I would expect from you, but allowable."

"I don't have it completely together," she said. They'd talked briefly about her masterful control of the office and everyone's schedules. He certainly wouldn't have survived without her background control of the little necessities that made his life simply work. "But I want to show you and the other guys that I'm worthy of taking on assignments beyond the reception desk."

So her plan for the week was to impress him? Done. Onto the next plan. Which was…? Locate the elusive relationship coach and charm him into becoming Asher's first official artist.

"Shall we?" she asked.

Asher realized he still held her hand. It felt like some kind of anchor to a reality he rarely touched. He wasn't sure if that was a good or bad thing. But something told him he was going to find out soon enough.

"Sure, honey," he said.

Maeve wrinkled her nose.

"Honey doesn't work for you? Babe?"

A vehement head shake.

"Sweetie, darling, lover?"

She cracked a terrified grimace.

"Just Maeve?"

She exhaled and nodded.

Just Maeve then. But not our Maeve.

How about *his* Maeve?

At check-in Asher played the suave boyfriend in dark sunglasses and a designer suit who sweet-talked the receptionist into a room facing the steaming geothermal springs behind the resort. Meanwhile, Maeve browsed the glossy flyer detailing the week's schedule. What was life without a proper schedule? Lots of classes, instructive sessions and spa moments but—what was that subtitle below the title of Reconnecting Romance? She'd not noticed that detail when booking tickets.

"It's late, but do you have time for the entrance interviews?" the receptionist asked. "They take about fifteen minutes and will help us to fine-tune your schedule for the week."

Asher glanced at her and shrugged.

Maeve grabbed his hand. "Just a second. I need to talk to my boss—er…boyfriend." With a forced smile to the receptionist, she then tugged Asher aside near the fountain bubbling in the center of the pristine Prussian-blue-tiled lobby.

"What's up, sweetie? Sorry. Maeve."

A momentary thrill of hearing him say her name swept through her like a cyclone, only to be followed by an even bigger, and more harrowing, disaster. "It's this." She waved the flyer between them. "This is not just a couples' spa vacation."

"What? The signs say Reconnecting Romance. Kind of cute."

"Right, it is a spa, and about romance, but it's

also focused on this." She turned the flyer toward him and tapped the top line.

Asher read, "Relationship *rehab*?"

Maeve swore under her breath. "I'm so sorry, I didn't notice this when signing up. I can't believe I let that slip by me."

"What does it mean exactly?"

"It means that not only are we faking being a couple, now we're going to have to fake relationship issues. We're here to *fix* our relationship, not relax and rejuvenate."

Asher winked at her. "Guess I'm calling you sweetie, after all."

He turned and told the receptionist they could do their interviews now.

CHAPTER THREE

MAEVE ARRIVED AT the room before Asher. She rolled in her suitcase and walked beyond the bed, dressed in natural linens, to the patio doors to look over the landscape. Other than her weekend strolls through Bishops Park, she so rarely saw unrestrained nature. Outside the room, lush forest hugged one side of the resort with emerald, olive, sepia and glints of azure, and a mossy rolling plain hissed with pearlescent steam billowing from various geothermal pools. The main pool behind the resort featured a wooden walkway circling it and a shower house.

The plan was to settle into that pool as quickly as possible. Though, she understood they'd have to attend the classes to not stick out and look like a pair of art brokers skulking about to find the reclusive owner. Reception had said they'd email a schedule within the hour. It was late, so she'd unpack and...

Turning, she took in the room. Much smaller than she'd expected for a luxurious resort. Just the one low platform bed. It did not offer a lot of stretching-out space. Not even queen-size?

"Bother," she muttered. What would she and Asher do about the sleeping situation?

There wasn't even a sofa or easy chair. Two wood stools were placed before a narrow natural wood bar situated to look out the patio windows. And on the wall opposite the bed hung a large mirror. A person could not lie in the bed or make any movements on it without having such motions reflected to them. Like a kinky—no, she wouldn't go there.

Well. She could, but she must not.

"Double bother."

Peering into the bathroom, she was relieved to see it was larger than most hotel offerings and featured a deep soaking tub, separate shower and two small mirrors above two sinks. About the same size as the bedroom.

"Weird," she decided of the setup.

Then she crossed her fingers that whatever was involved in a relationship rehab did not involve… She glanced to the mirror and shook her head. Not wise to think too far into that one. She was nervous enough now that she stood in this room, waiting for the one man she had admired for years.

More like ogled and secretly swooned at as he entered the office and filled the air with his easy charm and barest hint of intriguing cologne.

Asher Dane captured her attention with nothing more than that discerning crimp of brow and his innate confidence. And those stunning glacier-blue eyes that were framed by earthy brown hair. And while he always wore the most expensive suits, tailored to fit his tall frame, she did schedule gym dates for him twice a week, no matter what country or city he was in. When he called and listed off the various outdoor activities he wanted to try in his spare time while on a business trip, she'd look them up and schedule a session for him.

Maeve had been running Asher's life for the last two years, and he'd never even acknowledged it. Of course, he had a private life that she wouldn't attempt to dabble in. On the other hand, most of his life was posted to his social media pages. Accounts she wasn't allowed to handle. Fine with her. She'd seen enough of his *woman holding his hand and looking toward some fabulous sight* shots that she'd rolled her eyes so far back into her head there were days she wondered if they might get stuck. It was his thing. A gimmick. His followers always gushed and liked and hearted the posts. The women's faces were never shown. They were props in his art.

"Just another of his harem?" she muttered as she unzipped the suitcase and took out the book lying on top of her clothes. A copy of *A Natu-*

ral History of the Senses by Diane Ackerman. A dog-eared comfort read.

Never would she want to feel such a way while dating a man. So, yes, that confirmed her fantasies were simply that—dreams. The Face had shown her who he was—an egotistic attention-seeking influencer—and he wasn't her type.

Until she got to the cerebral and inner life of Asher Dane. The way he got lost in a painting...

She clutched the book to her chest and closed her eyes. So many times she'd found herself leaning over the back of her chair, chin in hand, as she'd watched Asher standing in the main conference room, alone but for a recent acquisition—whether painting, sculpture or antique—and realized he lost himself in the observation of another person's creation. It never ceased to thrill her, to give her a zing of shared appreciation and an even deeper swell of admiration for his passionate interest.

Maeve spun abruptly as the door opened and in walked the man of her daydreams. "Mr. Dane!"

She instantly adjusted her thrill level.

Don't act like the rest of the swooning women so happy to be in his presence. Just chill. Be normal.

As normal as a twenty-seven-year-old woman with a penchant for wild colors, copious daydreaming and a desperate need to increase her income could be.

He narrowed his gaze at her. She couldn't tell if that was a smirk or a curious smile. "Were you expecting someone else?" He made a show of looking around him as he rolled in his suitcase.

"No. You surp—doesn't matter. How did your interview go?"

He plopped his Louis Vuitton suitcase on the bed and sat beside it. "They wanted to know what one relationship issue we have that I didn't think we'd overcome while here. I mean, what? I don't even know you!"

"You didn't tell them that?"

"Don't worry. I can play the fake better than most." He lay back, stretching his arms out, and Maeve saw the bed was not going to fit them both comfortably. Was the size purposeful? Force the couple having relationship issues to sleep close?

Mercy, she was in too deep. Was it too late to run screaming for the safety of her tidy office files and accept her life would be forwarding phone calls from here on?

"I told them we're have trouble communicating," she offered, then tugged his suitcase from the bed and rolled it to the wall next to hers. "It's been rolling across the ground and the wheels are dirty," she offered to his silent query. "I figured that's what most couples have issue with, yes?"

"I suppose. Good call, Marsha."

She spun and gaped at him.

He winked. "You see? I already know what you're going to say to me. I'd say we're pretty good at communicating."

"Hmph. Every time you call me Marsha I'm going to call you Windfield."

"Where did that one come from? Sounds like a stiff-lipped butler."

"He was the principal at my primary school. It's a very pompous name."

"So you think I'm pompous?"

"No. It's just…" A tease. She didn't want to start out with an argument. This week was going to be stressful enough if they introduced real miscommunication. "I think we'll manage to convince them well enough that we're not on the same page." Her phone pinged, and, setting the book on the bed, she checked the screen. "Reception sent the schedule that starts tomorrow morning at six."

"Not going to work for me. My brain doesn't start functioning until seven or eight at best."

"Then you'll miss breakfast and…a crystal bowl chakra clearing."

Asher closed his eyes and smiled. "Bring me

back a cinnamon roll if they serve them. So what are we going to do about the sleeping situation?"

Maeve opened the closet and surveyed the contents. "There's extra blankets and pillows in here. I can sleep on the floor."

Asher sat up, regarding her for the first time since he'd walked into the room. His soft gaze tripped from her shoulders, down her skirt and then back up to what felt like her lips. Suddenly she felt unclothed. Like he could see every line of her body beneath the fitted dress and was calculating...things.

Things she wouldn't mind doing a few calculations on herself.

Seeming to catch himself, he inhaled and looked aside. "You think I'm going to do the chivalrous thing and argue that I wouldn't dream of allowing you to sleep on the floor?"

She could hope for as much. Maeve shrugged.

He made a show of considering it for far too long. "We can share the bed."

"Not a good idea. You take up the whole bed!"

"Yeah, but you're a pixie from the land of Eire." He tried for an Irish accent at the end of the sentence, and it set Maeve's heart to a flutter. "You'll only require a sliver of mattress."

She'd never imagined his attempt at an accent could affect her as if he'd touched her. Right there. On her—

"What's this book? You think you'll have time to read while here?"

Shaking out of a familiar fantasy, she took the book from him. "I never go anywhere without a book. But back to the bed situation, I'm a stretcher when I sleep. Arms out, legs this way and that. There isn't room for both of us in that bed." She tugged down the blankets and a pillow from the closet shelf and tossed them to the floor. "It's late, but I'm still a bit buzzed from the wine on the flight. I think I'll take a walk and check the outside amenities."

"Might I join you?"

Maeve twisted a look over her shoulder. He seemed genuinely interested in accompanying her. And what woman could honestly say no to those glacier blues? "I suppose that is what couples do."

"And we are a couple. I need to walk off the flight and decide whether to take the floor or the bed."

"Maybe we take turns?"

"Possible." He stood before her like a god rising from the depths to command the space and air around her, hair curled haphazardly about his ears and neck—his utter *presence* enveloping her.

Maeve sighed.

Asher quirked a brow, and then there was

that knowing wink. Darn it! She'd swooned, hadn't she?

"I'm going to wash up," he said with a nod toward the bathroom. "I'll meet you outside in ten."

"Sure." She pulled out a bright violet sweater from her suitcase, and squeezing by him in the narrow entry, she made it out of the room without another mutinous sigh.

For the next few days she was stuck in a small room that offered only a single bed, with the sexiest man alive. This was either going to be hell, heaven or the worst kind of crazy that would try her every nerve, erogenous zone and mental fortitude.

The sun shone above a stretch of volcanic lava that had hardened over decades to a craggy obsidian frosting. Steam rose up from geothermal pools of assorted sizes and locations across the landscape. The earth and air mixed a heady verdant scent that Asher realized he missed living in the city. The light here was ethereal, at times ineffable. Nature did things to a man. *It cured.* And he was in for the benefits.

"That sky view is not going to stay there forever. I have to get a shot."

He tugged out his phone from an inside suit coat pocket that his tailor had lined with protective material. While Maeve wandered to the railing that edged the vast walkway that meandered throughout the resort grounds, he lined up the shot. "Faking aside, we're going to have to hold hands for this. You've seen my shots." His followers loved the shots of a woman looking toward the scenery while he held her hand. They were sort of his trademark.

Maeve, her choice of purple and peach clothing inadvertently matching the sunset, crossed her arms and shook her head. "I'll pass."

Asher stared at her, agape, then realized his mouth was open and shut it.

"Much as I adore your eye for preserving the perfect shot," she added, "I don't want to be another faceless prop."

She wasn't to be… A prop? How rude. Why wasn't she as amiable as, well—the women in his photos were not… Hmm…

Very well. The fact that he never showed their faces *did* make them into a kind of prop. But they always consented. They understood his medium and were always thrilled to be included when he shared the photos with his followers.

The defiant curve of Maeve's lips softened and she shrugged. "There you go. We've established a relationship issue."

Meager, but it could be useful. Lifting his phone and framing the shot, he took a few, sans

Maeve, then turned off his phone and tucked it away. He hadn't plans to post anyway. They'd decided The Art Guys' followers didn't need to know that Asher was at a relationship retreat this week. There would be questions.

He didn't need those questions. The Face was all surface and no depth. And he preferred it that way.

"Your phone is never on," she noted. "I can't count the times I've tried to contact you and you never answer."

"It's…" The thing he'd learned to do after years of watching his parents suffer from the debilitating effects from radiation and electronic frequencies. Thus, the special protective material in his suit coat pockets, and turning off electronics when he wasn't using them. He wanted to be smart. And really, his life was busy enough without being a slave to the constant ring or ping of texts. "Just my way."

He willed her not to question him further. The last person he wanted to spill his guts to was the receptionist who already knew too much about his life as she organized his trips and daily life on the road.

"I've decided to only carry my phone when necessary this week," she said. "I did tell Krew and Joss I'd be available if they had issues. But I've emailed detailed instructions to each of them, along with a schedule, and I also set up daily phone alerts."

"You do like schedules," he noted without realizing that it could be an accusation.

Maeve lifted her chin. "What's wrong with being orderly and respecting others by being on time?"

Was that a dig? So he had a tendency to show up ten or twenty minutes late. Often.

"It's…" she continued. "I know how to do certain things and I like them done my way. Krew and Joss seem to appreciate my assistance."

"They do," he offered, knowing he'd cut her, and angry at himself that he'd done so. "As do I."

"You rarely give me a glance when you're in the office. And my texts go unanswered for days."

"But you always manage to get me to where I need to be and make my life easier for the details you attend to. I'm aware of all you do, sweetie." He winked then because it felt necessary to lighten the mood.

"Thanks, Windfield. I appreciate hearing that."

Touché. Well, they were headed in the correct direction—a couple in need of romance rehab—so he wouldn't let it bother him.

Asher crooked his arm toward her. "I noted the dining room is open all hours. How about we end the day with something decadent."

"More wine? Cheese and crackers?"

She hooked her arm through his, and he felt as if it were a gift he would be wise to tender carefully. He smirked at her simple pleasures. "I was thinking chocolate and Chantilly cream. I sneaked a look at the menu while on the flight. Thought to preplan an excursion or two. Are you in?"

"You said the magic word."

"Chocolate?"

"Preplan."

It had been a long day with the flight and the anxiety of learning they had to fake being an arguing couple. All Maeve wanted to do was take Asher's arm every chance she got and swoon over him. But to remain undercover they had to assume the ruse—or risk getting kicked out.

In the dining room, Asher sat on a cozy window seat, one leg stretched the length of it and leaning back to study the starry sky through the window that curved from over their heads down to the floor. His suit coat strewn aside, shirt cuffs and top two buttons undone, he raked his fingers through his earthy hair and looked absolutely...

"Stunning," he said.

"Yes," she agreed, and then caught herself in the daydream of tangling her fingers in his hair and inhaling him. *Pay attention!* Maeve glanced upward where he pointed. "Oh, yes, the stained glass." A half circle of stained glass topped the large window that dominated the farthest end of the dining room. It wasn't a scene but rather geometrical shapes in finely detailed arrangement. "The colors are amazing. Royal blue and eggplant. It's a bit too modern for your tastes, yes?"

"It is." A smirk crimped his cheek. Caught her mooning over him again?

Oh, Maeve, control yourself.

The plate she had propped on her lap held a half-eaten chocolate lava cake surrounded by an ocean of Chantilly cream. She'd eaten all the thick melty chocolate from the middle.

"So." She sat up straight and set her plate on the table. "What's our plan for…" She glanced around the vast dining hall. No cameras in sight, but one never knew. "…talking to you know who?" she whispered.

Asher swung his legs down and patted the cushion beside him. "Slide over, Margo, this sounds conspiratorial. And I do love some intrigue."

While she loved his fanciful nature, she still wasn't sure if his use of incorrect names was all in play or if he really didn't remember hers. He'd called her Maeve on the plane and once at reception. She'd give him a pass for now.

Sliding up beside him, she plucked up his suit coat in the process, folded it and carefully laid it over the back of the seat. Then she cast another look around the dining area, which was elegant and Nordic in design, while the space toward the front of the room was more cafeteria, walk-up and self-serve style. One other couple stood by the ice cream machine talking quietly.

When Asher leaned in she felt him sweep over her like warm sun. His scent, his body heat, his presence. It wasn't like cologne or spice, or any of the tired scents men wore. It smelled like royal violet swirled in earth and rain. She could imagine the color and thought it would suit him well, what with his lightly tanned skin and dark hair.

He whispered, "We are talking about Kichu, right?"

"Yes. And who knows if we're being watched."

"Gotcha. I can do the sly."

"I read the schedule." Lifting her chin straightened her body. The heat wafting from him shimmered through her being, teasing at her self-control. "All classes headed by Mr. Kichu are taught via Zoom. He only makes a live appearance on the final day."

"That's not going to work for us. We need to get to him sooner. Charm him."

"I'm going to leave the charming to you. I'm the student, remember? But you're right. We can't leave this until the last day. If he's so averse to selling his art, we need to work on him. And see the art. Is it even worth the effort?"

"All art is worth the effort."

"Even Mondrian?" she asked, knowing his utter disgust for the artist's works.

"Such basic colors. So…geometrical." The last word he spoke as if naming a foul substance.

Maeve laughed softly. She did share his penchant for the lush and beautiful. She didn't mind some of Mondrian's less geometric, landscape works, but the colors were *pedestrian*, as she'd once heard Asher state.

"We need to explore the resort, locate his private rooms," she suggested. "Maybe we'll catch him walking somewhere?"

"The resort is huge. Much bigger than I'd expected for the dozen couples staying. It could house hundreds. And there's an underground space. I noticed the drive going down toward the carport. There's a lot of area to cover."

"We can't be caught skulking about."

"Probably not, but if we go as a couple there's always the excuse that we got lost."

"A person can get lost on their own." Why was she trying to talk him out of sharing a sleuthing adventure? Any time spent with him racked up points in her fantasy.

He leaned forward to look at her. "I know you

don't need anyone to do your exacting and precise work, darling, but get into character, will you? Love of your life here, remember?"

If only he knew how true she wanted those words to be. And how difficult it was to fake being in love with Asher when really she was a little in love with him already, yet they were at odds, but not really, and, oh—this was getting complicated.

He took her hand and kissed the back of it. All the body heat she'd been feeling emanate from him now gushed from his lips to the back of her hand, infusing her with a giddy inhale. Though, she'd seen him perform the same chivalrous move many a time when introduced to a female client at the office. A tool in The Face's charming arsenal. But still, Maeve was pretty sure his atoms had permeated her skin to forever entangle in her molecular makeup.

"Relax," he said. "We've got this."

Oh, he had some part of her, that was for sure. *Please don't blush, please don't blush!*

"We do?"

"We'll case the joint early, before classes begin, and then again late after they've finished."

"Good plan. But you are not an early bird."

"For you, I'll set my alarm. And, you can have the bed tonight. I have occasion to sleep on the floor. It's good for my back."

"Are you sure?"

"I'm not sure about much, but I am sure about one thing. I need this artist to prove my worth to the other guys. And that will require your help." He stood and held out his hand for her to take. "You in?"

She clasped it. "I'm always in for secret spy stuff."

He tugged her to her feet and she tipped forward, catching her palm against his chest. They both looked to the couple by the ice cream machine, who did not notice their awkward and surprise embrace.

"Even couples having difficulties are allowed some intimacy," he offered.

His eyes traced hers, and she relaxed her curled fingers against his shirt, noticing that his heartbeat thundered under her palm. Maeve nodded, unsure what to say that wouldn't see her blurting "I love you!" like some lovesick teenager.

She didn't love him. She admired him. She respected his art aesthetic. And she fantasized about him in a manner that involved shedding clothing amidst tangled sheets. None of that required love.

He tipped up her chin and tilted his head in wonder. "So much in there."

"In where?" she asked innocently.

"Your eyes. They are like paintings. The light is…ever changing. And don't even get me started on your mouth. I like to…well…"

"You see stories in paintings," she rushed out.

"How do you know that?"

She shrugged. "I've seen you stand before a piece of art. I know that feeling. It's the best kind of lost."

"Lost in the story of the paint." He kissed the back of her hand again. "Best we be careful we don't graduate this rehab too quickly, eh, Penelope?"

Was he implying they were getting along? That they had a common interest? Of course they did, and why couldn't that be enough for him to fall to his knees, propose and live happily ever after with her?

Oh, Maeve! She told herself that she should be focusing on her own needs. She must do what she could to show Asher she was a valuable asset to The Art Guys so he could bring a positive report back to Krew and Joss. Increased wages meant the dream of her color consulting business could become a reality. She must not fail!

"Course not." She dropped his hand and smoothed a palm down her skirt. "Until you can remember my name, we've nothing to worry about, Windfield. I'm going back to the room for a shower. I'd appreciate you giving me ten minutes of privacy. I'll take the bed, as offered. See you in the morning?"

He called after her as she strolled off, "Remember, I like cinnamon rolls!"

Already feeling so at ease with her to request she serve him? The notion didn't bother her at all. She'd serve him sweets to sweeten his affections toward her. And she would also prove to him she knew her art, as well as what it was that pleased him. When it came to art, that is.

And maybe her?

Business before pleasure, she reminded herself. Mariane Pemberton would shake her head severely if she saw her daughter kissing up to the boss to gain momentum at work. A woman who relied on a man to achieve success would never truly be an independent force.

Maeve knew she could be that force. And she would find her way to her dreams this week. And if that required kissing up to the boss? Her mother would never have to know.

CHAPTER FOUR

THEIR EARLY-MORNING spy mission was dissuaded by a bright-eyed employee carrying an old-fashioned walkie-talkie. Maeve and Asher had slipped down a dimly lit hallway that didn't appear to lead to any guest-friendly parts of the resort. After they'd tracked in about fifty feet, Maeve realized someone else was in the hallway. She tugged Asher around, and they both looked the smiling employee in the eye.

"Just trying to find an exit," Asher summoned up the lie quickly. "I think we're lost, aren't we, sweetie?"

"I told you we should have turned left back there." Maeve tugged the small backpack the resort had provided over her shoulder. When she noted Asher held his hand open near her thigh she slipped hers into it. "Honey."

Asher's demeanor changed quickly. "You are always picking the wrong way. Why should I take your word?"

Shocked, but suddenly aware of what he was

doing, Maeve played along. "You never listen to me. You didn't even get my name right the first weeks we were dating!"

"Oh, come on, Marsha, don't be like that."

"Uh, I'll show you to the outer door," the young girl in green khakis interrupted. She twirled around, expecting them to follow. "The resort is a bit twisty at times. There's nothing down this way but storage rooms."

"He's always getting us lost," Maeve added as they rounded the turn and the obvious light from outside shone down the hallway. "Of course, that way."

They thanked the girl and headed outdoors. The employee called after them, "Stick with the program, guys! It'll get better! I promise!"

They walked outside to the brisk morning air, which would warm to a cozy seventy degrees before noon. Maeve wore a yellow sweater with tiny violets appliquéd around the neckline above ankle-length green-and-brown-striped chinos. Around her neck she had on a bright fuchsia scarf because the day had felt promising, if not daring.

"Failed," she muttered.

They wandered the wood pathway toward a vast patio area that overlooked a former volcanic field covered in a soft blanket of emerald moss. It bumped and cragged and dipped and curved. The terrain was very Seussian. Yet a sign warned them to stay on the path. Lava fields were fragile and sharp lava could be concealed by moss.

"Not a failure." Asher slung his suit coat over a shoulder, keeping it in hand with a fingertip. "We ruled out that section of the resort. We're narrowing down our options."

"You're quite the optimist, Windfield."

"I thought we managed that fake argument well."

"We did," she said with a big smile.

He met her renewed enthusiasm with a fist bump. "As for my optimism, it comes in handy when standing in an auction room vying against a determined bidder who wants the one item you need most."

"So it's optimism that nets million-dollar artwork?"

"Always. I rarely lose a piece."

"I think it's that patented charm of yours. You deploy that toward the opposing bidder and they lose all logic, forget what they're doing, and you win the bid."

"You think? Can't say I've tried it on a man, but the women…"

She knew he would be as successful charming a man as he was with the women. Asher had a unique appeal that she felt sure most would succumb to. She had, after all. The man had a certain ease that could make anyone feel comfortable, and that was a rare quality to possess, let alone utilize to one's advantage.

Herself, she tended to speak with her clothing and exacting work. She wasn't an extreme introvert. She liked to mingle and talk amongst small numbers of people. It was groups and intense conversations that tended to ratchet up her anxiety. Those were times when she wore jewel colors because they made her feel as if she wore a protective shield.

"I do have to give you credit for seeing me on my feet before seven in the morning." He strode ahead to a bench that overlooked a volcanic spring posted off-limits for bathing, and which captured the rising sunlight in a metallic sheen across its glossy surface. He sat and she joined him.

"It's because of this, isn't it?" She pulled out a box from her backpack and handed it to him. Breakfast was already available at the dining room.

Opening it, he lifted the oversize pastry to his nose to smell and chuckled gratefully. "Oh, you are good."

The cinnamon roll was so fresh it still steamed when he pulled it apart, and she could smell the sugary frosting.

"Did you bring one for yourself?" he asked as he bit into it and moaned with pleasure.

"You're not going to share?"

He paused in his enjoyment and studied the treat, then glanced at her. Was that actual indecision pulling at his face?

"Don't worry." She pulled out another box to reveal inside a fresh *pain au chocolat*. "I'm a chocolate girl."

They toasted with their pastries then sat quietly eating them. Maeve could get used to scenery like this. She'd always lived in a city. Had grown up in Dublin. Then moved to London. When she'd been a child, her parents would pack up the caravan every summer for a week and they'd head off on an adventure, seeing the sights across Ireland. Eagle Point in West Cork had been her favorite because her dad had taught her to fish there. But those blissful summer trips had ended when her mum had rocketed to investing mogul, divorcing Maeve's dad to fulfill her dreams.

Winners never fail, was one of the Mumisms that Maeve could never pry out of her bones.

Maeve had failed with her small business. And her mum wouldn't let her forget it.

Oh, Maeve, maybe now you'll do something sensible. Art is so…subjective. Ethereal. You belong in a solid job where you can rise through the ranks and prove yourself. Marketing, invest-ments, hell, even real estate. Forget about the silly color stuff. See where it got you? You need to apply yourself!

Which meant *prove* herself. Her mum tended to dole out her love and affection through gold stars and ratings for a job well done like some kind of online ordering service. Physical affec-tion was not in Mariane Pemberton's wheel-house. Likes and dislikes were.

"What are you thinking about?" Asher wiped his fingers on a napkin from inside the box.

That she needed to succeed without asking her mum for another loan.

Maeve set down her empty box. "This scenery is like a painting. It's got an amazing story to it."

"What story does it tell you?"

She closed her eyes, inhaling. Fresh green mixed with a dry rocky tone and a spice of salt from the ocean that was but an hour's drive away. When she opened her eyes, for a few sec-onds everything was more vivid. It was in that split-second fresh look she discovered so much in art.

"It's an old tale," she said. "Steeped in myth and legend but threaded through with truths." She caught herself in the mad fantasy that had been ingrained in her since she'd learned to read.

Most definitely a gene she'd inherited from her bookworm of a father. "Silly of me."

"No, it's not. I like your scenario for this place. Makes a guy imagine things."

"Like what?"

"Like fairy warriors marching along the horizon and ancient evils rising up from the bogs."

Enamored at the man's fantastical musing, she could only nod. Was there more to Asher Dane than being The Face for a billion-dollar art brokerage?

"I should snap a shot," he said.

Maeve's shoulders dropped.

"But I won't." He propped an ankle over his knee and leaned back to look at her. "I'll remember it. Can I ask you something?"

"Go for it." She took the box from him and nestled it in her lap, setting their refuse aside on the bench.

"I assume you don't have a significant other since you are here on this playdate with me. Can't imagine any boyfriend would be happy with such a situation."

"You assume correctly."

"Why is that?"

"What do you mean?"

"You're very pretty. You're smart. You seem to have your wheels on the track, heading in the right direction. What man wouldn't want to date you?"

Hearing her dateability assessment from Asher lifted her, but she wasn't going to read it the wrong way.

Just here on a fake date, she reminded herself. *Don't let your heart get involved.*

"I don't need to always be in a relationship to enjoy my life."

"Nor do I. But having someone to share life with does make it more fun. Interesting."

It did. Because had she been sitting here on the bench alone the landscape wouldn't have been quite so vibrant or her mood so light.

"I've recently had some bad luck on the dating front," she confessed. "I know it shouldn't put me off, and it doesn't, but I guess a streak of caution colors my life lately."

"Anyone who broke your heart never deserved the chance at it in the first place."

"That's very kind." And something a professional charmer would say. But, oh, to find a man who subscribed to such a platitude. "I broke off a relationship last year because the guy couldn't look up from his gaming console long enough to acknowledge I was there."

No matter what loud colors she had worn, she'd never broken through that man's wall. And she'd realized there was nothing she could do to her exterior to make herself pretty enough. A failure, certainly.

"I don't understand the preoccupation with those digital games," Asher said. "Some people literally live online. It's sad. And don't begin to compare getting lost in a painting to a computer screen, as one client insisted to me. They are not the same thing. Art is real. It lives and breathes. So much light there."

Maeve wanted to tilt her head against Asher's shoulder and revel in their shared outlook on art, but she wasn't that irrational.

"But you must date more often than yearly?"

She sighed. "The most recent guy… We went on one date. I thought it went well. We shared common interests. He was an avid cyclist, and I looked forward to getting back into biking should we see more of each other. We'd exchanged info. He'd promised to text me. Days went by and he didn't, so I texted him. I finally figured out he was ghosting me."

"That's rough."

"Guess I wasn't good enough for him either. Maybe it's wise if I stick with the fake dating, eh? No commitment. All the fun?"

"Have we had any fun yet?"

"I thought our spying mission was daring and adventurous."

"That was beginner level. It'll only get more exciting. Promise."

"I look forward to it. We have couples' yoga today. What's more exciting than that?" She caught him rolling his eyes. "I know. But we're playing our roles, yes? We'll go on another spy mission this evening."

"Yoga it is. And wasn't there something about pottery later this week? Such adventure."

His sarcasm was not lost on her. "I can switch it out for container gardening, if you prefer."

"Let's stick with the pottery. Maybe I can try my hand at recreating a Grecian vase. What I wonder is, how do all these crazy classes improve one's relationship?"

"I think it's to do with working together. Sharing experiences. I guess we'll find out."

"I enjoy spending time with you."

"You…do?"

He nodded and stood, seemingly unaware of her startled reaction. He enjoyed spending time with her? Same. But what did that mean? Was there the possibility they might become something more than workmates faking it?

"Of course," he replied and gestured that they walk toward the resort. "You always bring along the best treats." With a wink, he wandered ahead.

Maeve's shoulders dropped. As did her heart. So she was a mere receptionist here on vacation as well? Organizing his life in the background? Of course, nothing more than a fake.

Best she remember her position and focus on what she came here to accomplish. Showing Asher she was worthy of a promotion by helping him secure a new artist.

An individual class, divided by women and men, was scheduled before yoga. Maeve had been initially uncomfortable sitting amongst the dozen women in a circle, each with a notebook on their laps. The moderator had guided them through questions to ask about themselves, and they quietly scrawled notes.

Thinking this was going to be about her relationship with Asher—make that *fake* relationship— Maeve had decided she'd have to fake write as well. Until the questions came.

Are you proud of yourself?

Have you accomplished what you want to achieve?

What does your future look like?

With or without your partner?

Do you feel as though you rely on your partner for happiness?

Heavy stuff. But also, it did make her think. For a flicker in time, she had been proud of herself. She had accomplished what she'd set out to achieve. Opening the shop, along with Lucy, blocks down from where she lived. She'd had the rent paid for a year, the shelves had been stocked, the sign hung on the window. And then the pandemic had settled like a dark cloud over small businesses. That accomplishment had quickly turned to a failure that hung around her shoulders like a boulder on a chain.

Her mum had only echoed her failure.

You're my daughter. Where's the Pemberton ambition?

In there for sure, Mum.

But while Maeve was forward-thinking and focused like her mother, she didn't have the same energetic, almost maniacal drive to put herself into any situation that might see her advancing. She was more subtle, quieter. An introvert who could exist amongst the extroverts, but never truly peel away her colorful mask. Her inner world was nothing like the colors she wore on her body. This afternoon's soft heather yoga pants and mint paisley top echoed her eagerness to learn but also to not be seen. To blend into the foliage that surrounded the resort.

When the moderator instructed the women to look up from their notebooks, straighten and breathe, Maeve realized how hunched over she'd been. Literally curled upon herself as she'd scribbled *failure* and *try again* on the paper. She did need to breathe. To try again. As weird as

it seemed, this vacation was a chance for her
to prove to The Art Guys that she could take
on fieldwork. Which would provide the finan-
cial means to getting her one step closer to her
dream.

But was she ready for field work? Only once,
she'd held a paddle at an art auction. She hadn't
won; she suspected her boss had known that before even allowing her the task but had wanted to
give her the experience. She'd been a receptionist cum gallery attendant at that place. Hosting
gallery showings had taught her how to interact
with clients and to allow her art knowledge to
shine. She had only a year of art school under
her belt. However, she was capable. But she'd
not had the opportunity to put that knowledge
to real world use at her current job.

She and Asher needed to find and convince
Tony Kichu to sell his art. And—she had the
sudden thought—if *she* could be the person to
do that convincing it would go a long way in
showing her bosses she deserved a promotion.

In a manner, she was using this trip, and the
fake relationship with Asher, to get ahead. Her
mum would be so proud. Yet it didn't sit quite
right in a part of her.

Asher was using her as well. He needed to be
in a couple to attend this event and suss out the

elusive Tony Kichu. The man needed this win. It would be selfish to take it from him.

As if she even could.

Oh, Maeve, you are capable.

It's balancing that capability with the desire to see the one man she looked up to shine.

"That's a wrap, ladies! The couples' session begins in half an hour. Help yourself to refreshments at the back of the room."

The women swarmed to the fresh-squeezed juices and fruit jelly mooncakes, while Maeve wandered to the window that overlooked the moss and lava field that Asher had deemed worthy of a fantasy story. She wondered if he'd had to answer the same questions in his session. Now, there was a man who was proud of himself and his accomplishments. He'd never been shot down and forced to start from scratch. The Art Guys was a billion-dollar enterprise. She'd seen their balance sheet.

Though she was aware he'd had to leave the brokerage for a few years before they'd hired her. The office guys were hush-hush on the details behind that. It couldn't have been due to a failure. Asher had easily stepped back into the limelight and had taken on the role as The Face.

Asher deserved all the fame, accolades and social media likes that came his way, but she wondered if he ever felt as though something were missing. Had he accomplished what he desired? Was he fulfilled? Did he want a *real* relationship?

"I'll bring that to Tony," a voice sounded from across the room, alerting Maeve.

The moderator took an envelope from someone and left the room. Sparked by her desire to prove herself, and a hefty helping of intrigue, Maeve tucked her notebook into her backpack. Peeking out into the hallway, she spied the moderator and waited until she turned at the end of the long stretch of windowed hallway. Then she slipped quickly down the way and repeated her action, waiting for the woman to turn. She followed for a few seconds, when finally she heard an elevator ding. Rushing to spy the elevator doors closing, she saw that there were no floor numbers on the outer keypad.

"This has to be the way to the mystery man," she whispered with a smile. "Score."

He was not dressed for stretching out on a yoga mat. Suit coat abandoned and shoes removed, Asher sat cross-legged, facing Maeve, who also looked uncomfortable, but not because of her clothing. She could move with ease. Her dusty purple leggings and paisley green cropped top emphasized every slight curve on her petite body. The light in the window-walled two-story room was delicious, made even more interesting as it landed on Maeve. Her thick raven hair gleamed with traces of garnet and was pulled into a high ponytail. Those severe black bangs and lush long lashes seemed to glint in the light as if touched by fairy dust. And—mercy, those lips of hers. Bow-shaped, deep cherry smoothing to a darker crimson. Hugged by apostrophes. They were quickly becoming an obsession of his.

The last thing he'd obsessed over was winning a bid on an oil painting by Pre-Raphaelite artist John Everett Millais. *Ferdinand Lured by Ariel* had been part of a private collection suddenly put up for auction. Asher had bid against museums, dealers and unrevealed collectors calling in across the globe. That day he'd spent more money than he had on any previous auction— his client's money, that is. He'd been given the opportunity to sit with the painting depicting a scene from Shakespeare's *The Tempest* for nearly an hour before the transfer team had arrived to box it up and ship it to Romania, the country it now called home.

Maeve's lips were more compelling than that painting's mysterious green sylph whispering in Ferdinand's ear. Whatever she whispered? He would listen.

This class was called Heart Chakra Trust.

And while they waited for everyone to get into position, he leaned forward and asked Maeve, "What's a heart chakra?"

"It's right here." She placed a palm over her breasts at the center of her chest.

"And what does it do?"

She smiled. "It's the place where love resides."

"I knew that." He sat back, upright, wrists on his bent knees. "Good, then. Let's get on with this."

The sooner they finished this obnoxious exercise, the faster he could remove himself from this strange situation and go in search of Kichu's private apartments. He didn't mind the fake relationship, but he'd not expected classes where he had to examine his emotions and inner pride, like the all-male class he'd been in earlier. That sort of stuff was safely locked and sealed. Though, he had stalled on the *Are you proud of yourself?* question. Proud of using his good looks to move ahead in the world? Hardly.

Yet, how to step away from the mask and be the real Asher Dane? Some days he wasn't even sure who that man was.

"Class, we're going to engage in an exercise in trust and quiet acceptance this morning. Everyone move closer, bracketing your legs to the sides of your partner's hips."

Shuffling on the mats and a few hisses of annoyance accompanied Asher's hesitation. He looked to Maeve, who appeared flustered and unsure. The move would place them in a position he rarely even assumed with a lover.

He playfully nudged her calf. "For the fake, yes?"

She nodded. "Of course."

They gently moved toward one another until they had about a foot of space between their chests. Maeve's legs draped over his, and he relaxed his to either side of her hips. To say he could feel the sexual charge between them was not a lie. How could a man, any man, position himself so close to a woman and not feel some desire? And that he already found himself passionately obsessed with her lips did not make the situation any less awkward.

There was something so otherworldly about Maeve. And yet, not? She was…earthy. But also beyond.

The thought flashed Asher's memory back to an art history professor who had insisted Asher would never succeed in the art world because he was too surface level. He needed to get earthy and ugly. To dig his fingers into art and let it subsume him.

Earthy and ugly disturbed him. Unless it was packed in cherry red lips and mismatched patterns and colors. Maeve was the furthest from ugly. And her beyond-comprehension earthiness was irresistible.

"Now," the instructor said in a soothing voice as she walked amongst the couples positioned on mats around the sun-drenched room, "place a palm on your partner's heart chakra."

Maeve lifted her hand and asked, "May I?"

"Of course." She could touch him whenever she liked. Though he sensed her nervousness. Out of his peripheral vision, Asher could see the other couples doing so, some reluctantly.

When Maeve's hand landed softly on his chest it felt as though he'd been blasted by a magical force that surged through his body and electrified every part of his being. He'd been zapped by an earth witch who wore secrets on her lips.

And he liked it.

"You can put your hand on me," she suggested shyly.

Shaken out of his wonder, he lifted his hand and held it near Maeve's chest. The top she wore was cut to just above her breasts. Not overly large or too small. Just the right size. He'd have to rest the heel of his hand on them... It felt intrusive, and he didn't want to force the touch on her simply because they were playing at being a couple.

All of a sudden she took his wrist and pressed his palm to her chest. "It's okay," she said. "I'm a big girl. I know what we're doing here."

Right. Just faking it. But…really? This touch did not preach removed observation to him.

The instructor called, "Now, rest your foreheads against one another, and close your eyes. Simply feel your partner's breath. Their heartbeats. Their beingness."

A hush fell over the room. Asher looked to Maeve, who smiled sweetly then bowed her head forward, which he reciprocated. With his forehead touching hers in another zap of bright energy, he closed his eyes and whispered, "We can do this."

"No talking!" the instructor called. "This is a silent communion of your souls."

Justly admonished, he took some solace from Maeve's suppressed giggle. It was silly, their position, palms to each other's chests and foreheads touching. But also…

Maeve's warmth and softness permeated his skin. The faintest scent of vanilla was not like perfume, but rather as if it exuded from a plant in a wild jungle. Raw and dark and a little like Maeve herself. Her breaths moved his hand against her breasts. A strand of her hair tickled his chin. Their noses almost touched, but he tried not to let that happen. Because there were too many sensory alarms going off in him. Touching Maeve was anything but calm inducing.

Yet, the longer they sat there, the subtle throat

clearings and bodies shifting around them faded, and it grew into an intimate moment of just the two of them. Maeve's heartbeat thrummed against his palm. It slowed, growing calmer. Relaxing.

Did she trust him? She could. He would never do anything to harm Maeve. How did she feel sitting so close and touching him? Could she possibly move beyond the fakeness of all of it and step into the role of…?

His lover? A girlfriend?

Asher wasn't sure why that thought had arisen. He didn't want an involvement with Maeve.

Did he?

Oh, we know.

Maybe he did desire something more with Maeve. *Our* Maeve?

His Maeve.

Sensing she sat still with eyes closed, breaths measured, Asher had to suppress the intriguing thrill of whispering, "What are you feeling right now?"

Did she feel the electrical surge that seemed to move from her fingers through his chest and down his wrists, rocketing up his arms and to his chest? His entire body warmed, and it wasn't from exertion. He knew this feeling. The instant shock of attraction and—desire.

Maeve was not his type of woman. She was not tall and curvaceous. She did not style her hair and primp her face with cosmetics designed to draw the eye. Though her red lipstick always hit him right in the—well, *that* erogenous zone. She was dark and mysterious. Quiet on the inside. Yet she bathed herself in color. Beautiful but strange. She wasn't compelled by trends, or even matching colors. She was simply different. And so compelling.

Suddenly a whistle blew, and the instructor announced, "Kiss alert!"

The couples all looked to one another for explanation, and the moderator, with a laugh, explained that occasionally throughout the week a whistle would be blown. That indicated the couples should kiss. An effective means to reestablishing connection. There was no right or wrong, just that they made an attempt, even if they were angry with one another.

Asher looked to Maeve, whose expression bordered on horror. "We don't have to," he said. "It's…"

It was what? Crazy to want to kiss a woman he was attracted to? Not at all. Though, to do so in front of others, and for the first time, did feel uncomfortable.

And Maeve's look screamed *Get me out of here!*

"This is weird," she muttered. Their hands were

still pressed against one another's chests, their heads still close. "I mean, I like weird things."

"Is that so?" He'd suspected as much about her. "I can make it weirder."

With that assumed permission, Asher kissed her quickly. A smack to her lips. He barely had a second to register the connection. To wonder if she'd closed her eyes. To decide whether the apostrophes crimped even deeper or smoothed away.

Maeve sat back and touched her mouth. Her wide eyes were...not smiling.

Asher swore under his breath. "I'm so sorry. I shouldn't have..."

"Please don't apologize for a kiss," she pled, and gripped one of his hands. "That'll make it even weirder." She looked around. One couple was still engaged in a kiss. The others were gathering their mats to return to the cubbies.

"It's what needed to happen. Sorry—" He caught his mistake. "I mean... Right. It's part of the fake. Uh... Let me help you up." He took her hand and together they gathered and rolled up the mats.

What had he done? He shouldn't have—and yet, he couldn't regret it because that wasn't his style. He'd done it. He hadn't even taken a moment to feel it, to really enjoy her mouth...

He should have paid more attention!

On their way out of the gymnasium, Maeve shouldered up beside him but didn't say anything. What to say to a surprise kiss that hadn't been asked for? That she might have construed as an affront? Might she have liked it?

Asher raked his fingers through his hair and blew out a breath. "Whew! That was unexpected."

So intense. And not even in a sexual way. With his hand over her heart, he had connected with Maeve. Until that stupid whistle spoiled the moment.

"It was weird," she said, "but I'm not upset about it. In case you thought you did something wrong."

With that, she walked ahead of him, heading toward the dining room.

Not upset? Whew! He'd taken a chance. It had been for show. But really? He'd wanted to kiss her. And while it had been no more than a second of physical contact, he had felt the electricity between them.

Next time—and he hoped for that next time—it wouldn't be but a flash.

CHAPTER FIVE

"It's up ahead around the corner." Maeve was distracted by Asher's violet, rainy scent as they slinked down the darkened hallway. It was deep and lush and made her want to lick him in inappropriate places on his body. And she wasn't even standing that close to him. His scent had literally infused itself into her pores during the chakra class, and she now carried him on her.

What that session had inspired in her libido!

She had felt Asher to her very core. Yet that feeling had gone beyond mere sexual desire to wanting to reach in and see if she could touch his soul. To push aside his outer shell and breathe in the inner wonder that she knew resided within. A wonder she'd witnessed as he'd gotten lost in a painting. One that was burgeoning as she got to know him better here at the retreat.

But she mustn't read too much into that intimate ten minutes in which they'd been so close some religions might insist they immediately marry.

And then that silly whistle! She wasn't offended that he'd kissed her quickly. It was the apology for the kiss that still bothered her. Sure, he was being a gentleman and trying to go along with the instructions while also not intruding on her too intimately. They had been playacting, after all.

She mustn't allow her heart—which had been touched by Asher—to forget that. Because her focus was on getting ahead and gaining notice from her bosses. But not *that* kind of notice.

"Good job on the spying," he said as he pressed his back to the wall and then dared a look around the corner. "Clear."

The elevator dinged, and he suddenly grabbed her hand and skirted her back down the hallway in the direction they had come. They just made the corner as someone walked right by the spot where they had been standing.

Maeve's heart thundered. Asher still held her hand. Did he realize that? She clutched it, not wanting to let go. Hoping to restart that intense chemistry that had ignited between them on the yoga mat. Who cared about a spy mission? She was holding The Face's hand!

"Must be housekeeping. They're pushing a cart. Let's abandon this mission for now." He let go of her hand and directed her toward the main hallway that would lead to their room. "I'll take a look tomorrow morning."

"We've got more classes in the morning."

"Please, no more chakra touching."

"You didn't enjoy that session?"

"I..." He paused and took her in. If a look could feel like a hand over her heart, his did so. Falling into his eyes was not a hardship. And she didn't care anymore if she did blush. "I did enjoy it. It was intense. But as you can see from my outfit, I didn't pack for extracurricular floor activities. And what was up with that kiss whistle?"

She was glad he'd brought it up. That apology! Way to spoil the moment!

"It'll happen again," she said. "It took us by surprise. We should have planned for something like that."

"Who plans to be suddenly forced into intimacy with another person at the shrill peal of a whistle?"

"We were already deep into intimacy before that whistle."

"True. It was different, yes?" He moved along to walk slightly in front of her, turning to walk backward. "I mean it was so... I don't know how to describe it. It felt... You know."

Was he implying that he'd felt the same as she had? That it had gone beyond a sexual touch and into that soul-touching moment the instructor had implied could happen?

"I know," she agreed, hoping they were talking about the same experience. Maeve chuckled as they neared their room door. "It's okay. It was part of the fake. I didn't mind the kiss." Quick as it had been. Could next time be a little longer? Pretty please?

He paused before the door with the key card in hand, his eyes searching hers. "You sure?"

She nodded. "We can kiss again the next time the whistle blows."

"Like trained seals?"

She hadn't thought of it that way. Was he really put off by having to kiss her?

"Sorry." He slashed the card and pushed the door open to allow her to wander inside. "I generally don't kiss a woman without permission. It was awkward. Felt intrusive."

"So you want to fake it next time? Put our heads close and...? Nothing?" She shrugged. "Weird."

"You said you liked weird."

"I do, but I'm getting the feeling it's too weird for you. If you have something against kissing me—"

She turned to find he stood right there. She had to adjust her position a few inches backward. Tall, imposing, yet smelling like earth and rain.

She couldn't read his mood. Was he angry, confused, bordering a dull mossy green? Unwilling to kiss her again? She hadn't expected a relationship out of this adventure, and they had agreed to fake it. However, most couples *did* kiss.

"I don't want you to think that I kiss like that all the time," he finally said. "It was a reaction. But if I have your permission, in the future I promise that any whistle alert will see that you get properly kissed."

Maeve's jaw dropped open.

Asher touched her under the chin and pushed her mouth closed. His patented charm twinkled in his eyes. "I'll take that as permission."

"It is," she said quickly, then inwardly kicked herself for unloosing her silly desperation. "I mean, of course, we're just trying to make things look good. A proper kiss is what is required to show them we're a couple."

"Good, then." He walked around her to his makeshift bed on the floor and grabbed some things from his suitcase. "My turn at the bathroom first. I did think to bring along swim trunks."

They had plans to soak in one of the geothermal pools. A delicious reward for an awkward yet fulfilling session of touch, sudden kisses and intrigue.

CHAPTER SIX

THERE WERE STRICT rules for entering the natural hot springs located behind the resort. A thorough shower and scrub—naked—in the shower rooms. Maeve slipped on her one-piece, which was a bright mixture of primary colors, and wandered out to claim one of the half dozen small pools unoccupied by another couple.

The pool, formed by seismic activity, was about three feet deep, lusciously warm and fringed with the scruffy turf that coated the manicured grounds. Sulphur tinged the air, but it had to compete with the verdant foliage and the fresh air unhampered by city fumes and pollution. Flat stones were placed here and there around the edge, obviously to set things on. Sinking into the hot springs defined bliss. The water was a fusion of shades from sky blue to dusted turquoise and a deeper fir green. The steam rising would give her a good facial, that was for sure.

After settling deep into the warm water, she

was startled by Asher's approach. He ran toward the pool, looking ready to dive in. She put up a palm to stop him—

He froze at the pool's edge. Flashed her a charming grin. Then slowly lowered himself into the pool. Mercy, the man... Had. A. Physique. Those workouts she scheduled for him certainly paid off. Indulging in the eye candy of abs and pecs—how those muscles strapped his body and moved as if choreography with every step he took.

He closed his eyes and tilted his head against the smooth-edged stone. "Now, this is how a man takes advantage of a work trip. You like?"

Oh, did she like.

"I plan to come out here every day," Maeve said. "Twice if possible. I don't think I've taken a vacation."

Asher settled across from her in the pool. Their legs paralleled one another. The eight-foot-wide pool was as cozy as a hot tub.

"Ever?" he asked.

She shrugged. "Not since I was a kid. We would pack up the caravan every summer and visit our relatives and any national park we could find."

"I do love your Irish brogue. Faint, but it's colorful. What made you decide to move to London permanently? Why not Ireland?"

Because Ireland, while steeped with child-hood memories, was merely a birthplace to her. She had no friends or close family there now.

"Our last vacation was right before my grad-uation. It was the trip that Mum and my da de-cided to tell me they were getting a divorce. Mum is a go-getter, and she had turned Da's ex-pectations of what a wife should be on its head. He wanted her to wear an apron, cook, clean and greet him with a smile when he got home from work. She felt trapped and held back. And had begun to make a splash in the investing world. So they split."

"I'm sorry. Divorce must be rough for a kid."

"If I had been younger, I think it would have gutted me. Even at eighteen the experience was rough. But I've come to realize they do still love one another in their own ways, yet living to-gether wasn't possible for them. Da loves his slightly bohemian, devil-may-care lifestyle. And Mum loves the challenge of obliterating the cor-porate ladder. Also, she moved to New York City that autumn. She loves the US."

"And you? What location do you prefer?"

Maeve shrugged. "I'm easy. London is lovely but expensive. But so are cities in the States. And Ireland doesn't call to me in any meaning-ful manner. I guess I prefer the place where I can put down roots and build my own business."

"And what sort of business do you intend to build?"

"I had a business. Opened it exactly one month before the pandemic. I don't have to tell you how difficult it was for small businesses, especially new ones without a lot of marketing and buzz, to survive at that time."

Asher shook his head. "Didn't last?"

"Two months in we had to close up shop."

"We?"

"My flatmate, Lucy, and me. And we were never able to come back from that. I had to liquidate and sell everything to pay my mother back for the loan she gave me."

The failed shop had sucked up all her savings. She'd immediately handed over the money from what she'd been able to sell to her mum to cover the loan. And had received a warning that she must succeed. All Pemberton women succeeded at their endeavors.

Not all Pemberton women had lived through an economically devastating pandemic when trying to start a business.

Still, it was difficult to brush off her mother's disappointment. And she didn't intend to. She would rise again.

"That's rough. I'm sorry," Asher offered. "And then you found The Art Guys? I want to say I'm happy that your business closed because had it

MICHELE RENAE   89

not, you'd never have landed with us, but that doesn't sound so positive as it should."

"I'll take it. I needed the work, and I did study mixed arts at Westminster, along with night classes for business. The Art Guys is a good place for me. For now."

"You still have dreams of owning a business? What sort of business was it you had?"

"A color shop. We called it Fuchsia."

"And what does a color shop sell?"

"Color! We sold paints, pens, markers, paper, decorative items, everything a person could utilize to add color to their home. My goal was to eventually start a consulting service where I, acting as a color therapist, could redo a person's home or specific room by adding color to it. It's my thing."

"Apparently it is. I don't think I've ever seen you in subdued grays or blacks."

"I know my clothing isn't to your taste."

Asher made show of gaping at her.

"I've seen the way you look at me, a little confused, sometimes shocked. My fashion sense isn't for everyone. I tend to express myself through color." Unlike her mother, who wore the subdued grays and blacks like a religion.

"Your fashion is strange to me. But it's also intriguing. Like you're a puzzle that needs to be solved."

Maeve had never heard herself described that way. She liked it. Not quite readable on the surface, but if a person spent a little time sorting through her pieces…?

She slyly turned to look over Asher's relaxed face. His hair was a masterpiece of tease, the curly brown locks demanding a woman run her fingers through it. So handsome. And kind, even if he was a bit self-centered. It was because he was so focused on his work. And maybe some entitlement too. He had worked hard for his money and deserved every cent. The money didn't appear to corrupt him. He didn't own a splashy sportscar that she was aware of, and nor did he own a castle or flash bling on his wrist. He kept a small apartment in London—she knew; she authorized the monthly pricey rent payments for him—because he traveled all the time and hadn't the need for a real home. His focus was on art and putting it out there for the world to appreciate.

"So have you always lived in London?" she asked. She recalled their briefing on the flight here. "Did you say your parents moved to Bath?"

"Yes. My parents…they have been ill for a good portion of my life."

"Oh, I'm sorry."

"But they're doing better now. The move was what they needed."

He didn't seem to want to expound. Was that the reason he'd been forced to leave The Art Guys? She knew he'd taken extended time off before she'd been hired, but she didn't know why.

Teasing her lower lip with a tooth, Maeve vacillated on asking him.

"What?" Asher prompted. "I know you've got something burning in there, Marsha."

She didn't mind the stupid name. It was starting to feel like an endearment. Their own pet names for one another. Marsha and Windfield. Happily ever after.

Oh, Maeve. Get your head in the game!

Because this was just a game.

"I was pondering whether it would be okay to ask about your parents' illnesses?"

"It's…" He tilted his head against the turfed edge of the pool. His hair glistened with water droplets, and his muscled shoulders rose like tiny islands from the water. "It sounds crazy to most people, so I generally keep it private."

"Oh, I don't want to intrude."

"Let's talk about you." He leaned forward, floating his arms before him. "That swimsuit you're wearing is totally Maeve with the bright colors. Though it does echo shades of Mondrian."

She laughed. "I know! Not your favorite artist. I like the color blocking. The green gives me energy, and the blue is grounding."

"That's interesting. I've heard you refer to the colors as an emotion. What is it with you and color?"

If the man could see her London flat he would understand. Or go mad from the utter craziness of it.

"Let's say," she said, "I have a ridiculous obsession with color."

"Ah!" He assumed a dramatic tone and quoted, "'Thank you for curing me of my ridiculous obsession with love.'"

"You love *Moulin Rouge* too?"

"One of the best musical movies I've seen. And it is certainly color drenched. So have you always been into color?"

That he shared her favorite movie was exciting. And intriguing. He wasn't the sort she'd expect to enjoy such a wild, bohemian movie, and a musical at that. If she could have pinned a favorite movie to him she may have guessed something a little more action intense.

"I'd say so," she said. "As a kid I was always coloring and painting my things. I'd get teased in school because my trousers didn't match my shirt. I didn't care. It's how I express myself. Over the years that obsession turned into the desire to share my fascination with others."

"Thus, the color shop."

"Exactly."

"Well, I hope you can find that dream again. But as I've said, if that means losing you at The Art Guys then I won't hope too hard."

"I was thankful to find this job at the height of the pandemic madness." She recalled the guys mentioning that their previous receptionist had quit for fear of catching something—anything—and had become a literal hermit. "Though, you must know I've spoken with Krew. I'm looking to move up and possibly earn a raise from you guys."

"Anything can happen."

"You think?"

"Yes, but I mean, we are known as the Art *Guys*."

Maeve nodded. Had she expected to be included in such an exclusive club? Perhaps. She simply needed a means to make more money so the dream Asher half hoped could come true for her could be accomplished.

"I get it." She fanned her steam-moistened face. "I've no field experience with The Art Guys to prove myself."

"You have to start somewhere. If the art business is really what you are interested in, I'm sure we can figure something out. But I sense your color shop is more in your wheelhouse."

"It is. But I'm losing Lucy as a flatmate next month, and I'm beginning to feel a little desperate—oh. I shouldn't have said that."

"I understand, Maeve. If we're not compensating you properly for your much appreciated work, I'll have a talk with Krew."

"The pay is fair. For a receptionist. But my dreams will never come true unless I start earning more. I've considered trying my hand at influencing, like Lucy does. She does makeup tutorials and—you wouldn't believe the cash she earns from that."

"Perhaps you could do color tutorials?"

"I've considered that. But I'm not a camera girl. There's a reason I avoid the camera crew on filming days. I don't possess the charm and unabashed ease that you do. It's necessary to be an influencer."

"I like you as you are. Though I've wondered if your quiet manner was because I've done something wrong."

"What?"

He shrugged. "You never meet my gaze when I'm in the office. And your smiles are so rarely directed toward me."

"Oh. I…" Was only ever trying not to swoon over the man! And here she'd thought him a bit standoffish as well, never trying to make conversation with her! "I'm not offended by anything you've done. Trust me."

"Good to know. We make a great team, eh? That spur-of-the-moment save we did this morning when we were discovered was spot-on."

"For someone who favors honesty, I did find lying along with you a bit too easy. This whole trip is a big lie."

"It's an adventure, Maeve. Look at it that way. And we may even learn something about ourselves along the way."

"Like how to connect with another person's heart chakra?"

"That was a weird session."

"It will get weirder. We have pottery hugging on the schedule."

"I can't imagine what that will entail."

"I can. And it sounds kinky."

Asher's laughter was throaty and deep. Joining in with him felt natural, and Maeve was able to brush aside the fact that she'd revealed her selfish desire to make more money by accompanying him here. Just enjoy the holiday? She could do that. Because she was learning more about the man who she'd crushed on for years.

Asher moved to the center of the pool and leaned in. "Don't look now but everyone is staring."

Maeve had to force herself not to scan the

other pools where couples were bathing. "Do you think it's odd that we're laughing?"

"No, I don't—oh. Right. We're supposed to have issues. Hmm, good call, Marsha."

"Because you never get the directions right," she admonished, but playfully.

"Oh, yeah?" He splashed as he moved backward and pushed up to sit on the turf edge of the pool. "Well, you—" his voice raised with each word "—are always doing that—" he stood and then gestured to the sky "—that thing!"

Maeve caught his quick wink and realized this was another play. And she was in for the match.

"Oh, I'll give you a thing! That thing is—" she levered herself out of the pool and grabbed a towel "—something you will never understand!"

Out the corner of her eye she noticed a woman in one of the pools nod in solidarity. *Right, girl, you tell him.*

"I can't even look at you right now." Asher turned and marched away.

Realizing she would need to follow to get to the same door, Maeve did follow, stabbing her finger in his wake. "Maybe if you spent more time looking at me!"

Where that one had come from, she didn't know. A crazy thing to say. But she was acting right now.

Suddenly Asher turned at the edge of the grounds

where the lawn met the back patio. His eyes were fiery. The water droplets on his body glistening. Who could ever be mad at such a fine specimen of man?

"I'm always looking at you," he said so quietly that only they two could hear. "But you never seem to notice."

With that, he marched inside the resort.

Maeve lowered the hand in which she held the towel. His words had entered her chest as if he'd forced them in with mere thought energy. She *did* notice him. Always.

But he'd always looked at her?

Was that a part of the act or had he been speaking a truth just now?

CHAPTER SEVEN

ONCE OUT OF a quick shower, Asher tugged on a plush robe and wandered past the small bed and onto the patio. The evening had provided focused classes for individuals on recognizing emotional signals in their partner and understanding love languages. It had been…more interesting than he'd expected. He'd had taken a quick meal in the dining hall with the other men and then they'd returned to another class on personal growth.

Maeve arrived in the room and veered immediately into the bathroom. He hadn't seen her since their soak in the hot spring. Had he inadvertently offended her during their impromptu argument? Hurt her?

Of course he had. He'd just taken a class that had taught him to recognize an upset woman.

He hadn't meant to yell at her. It had been part of the fake relationship. But that last statement—that he'd always noticed her—had been a truth that had slipped off his tongue.

The woman had scratched his surface. A surface that was clean and polished and made to charm others. The Face. How he hated that moniker at times. The Face wasn't concerned with how he made others feel, because he had developed a patented charm that generally left those in his wake smiling.

He'd certainly not been so shallow and egotistic when he'd started the brokerage with the guys. It had all seemed to explode out of him after he'd returned following the years away to care for his parents.

The Face would never yell at a woman, be it fake or otherwise. And The Face would most certainly never expose his real feelings to a woman.

Or have to wonder if he'd hurt her.

An apology to Maeve was necessary.

What a crazy trip this was turning out to be. He'd never expected the emotional aspects of it all. That he would struggle with his attraction to their receptionist as much as he was. But, yes, he was attracted to her. And with the two of them sleeping in a room together, it seemed like a perfect time to explore that attraction.

But what would Maeve think about such exploration? Was he merely reacting to his own libido? His pattern was always the same. See a pretty woman. Discover if she was interested.

Kiss. Sex. So long. On to the next one. Was this the same thing again?

Something told him this was different.

And that awful kiss! It had been so quick. Forced. Unpracticed. And though she'd said she hadn't minded, he did. Never would he kiss a woman like that. He truly did want to show her what a proper kiss from Asher Dane was like. Which led him right back to his consternation that he was attracted to his receptionist.

Had he always been so? Sure, it annoyed him that she'd not paid him the proper attention whenever he stopped into the office. Was that because…?

"You really are interested in her," he muttered.

Startled by a commotion behind him, Asher turned to find Maeve standing in the open patio doorway, one foot dangling over the doorjamb. She'd changed into summery green striped pajama shorts and top that were speckled with bold red flowers. A crime against any artistic aesthetic, but apparently her means of expressing herself. What did the stripes and roses say about her mood right now?

"You can take the bed tonight," she offered.

"I won't think of it. It's yours. The floor is good for my back, as I've said."

"I don't believe one word of that. But…I'm done arguing with you for the night."

"Maeve, please." He rushed to her. "You know that was a fake argument back at the pool?"

She nodded. "I know. We're playacting. I'm just…" She faked a yawn against the back of her hand and turned. "It's been a long day. Those evening classes fried my brain."

"It's been a lot to take in."

Asher caught her hand and stepped across the threshold. He wanted to pull her into his arms, but it felt intrusive, too possessive. Despite the class, he couldn't read her emotions right now. She could be tired. Yet he intuited part of her had been offended by their argument, nonsensical and as fake as it had been.

"Some of what I said wasn't fake," he said softly. "About always looking at you." He winced. "Does that sound creepy?"

She chuckled softly and sat on the bed. "A little."

"I mean, I see you, Maeve. You're…beautiful." And a little strange. "You're smart and you have your finger on the office operations. We couldn't run as smoothly without you on our team. But me as well. I seek your approval, a glance, a smile, when I'm in the office, because…"

How to put this when he was just working all this out for himself?

"I like you?" he finally said.

She tilted a doubtful look at him. "Are you asking me or telling yourself?"

"I mean…well, yes. I like you. In a completely non-receptionist way."

"Oh." She nodded. It didn't seem apparent that she would respond in kind. Did he need her to? Probably.

But sometimes they want the acknowledgment.

Something he'd only learned today.

What was going on with his thudding heart right now?

"Good, then."

Now that he'd confessed that crazy, surprise desire, he was suddenly more nervous than he'd ever been around a woman. Asher fled for the patio and leaned on the railing. Behind him he heard Maeve climb between the sheets, punch her pillow a few times and settle.

He liked her?

That was the truest thing he'd spoken since arriving here at the resort. Stupid emotion classes! The woman had indeed scratched his surface. And he liked what had been revealed beneath.

CHAPTER EIGHT

ASHER WASN'T SURE how hugging was going to be incorporated into this pottery class. He and Maeve stood before a pottery wheel working cool wet clay into what they hoped would resemble a vase. Their creation was no small mantel tchotchke. This vase would hold volumes. Why had they been given so much clay?

Couples shared a wheel, and the instructor had specifically stated that unless they'd been spinning clay for decades, they shouldn't try any maneuvers related to the movie *Ghost*. That never worked, and they didn't need the mess.

He agreed that standing behind Maeve and manipulating the clay by moving her hands would feel awkward. Not that he wouldn't mind nuzzling his face into her hair. Romantic thoughts about Maeve came easily. It was the way her fingers slid through the wet clay and artfully worked to shape the vase. She was so intent, thoughtful. And when she caught his glance, her smile would brighten. She hadn't smiled at him so much in the entire two years she'd been working for him. His entire body warmed and the world felt right.

Hell, he needed to focus. But something distracted him when he heard a couple off near the back of the room muttering about Kichu's art.

Taking his hands from the vase and leaving Maeve to work her magic, Asher dipped his fingers in some water and took his time wiping them on the thick canvas apron he'd been provided while he focused on the conversation behind him spoken in whispers. The man speaking seemed to be aware that Kichu made art—and he was here to see it?

Daring a look over his shoulder, a sudden stab of recognition struck Asher painfully in his gut.

He turned back to the spinning vase. Maeve cast him a clay-smudged smile. But his focus remained behind him on the man talking about Kichu's art. What was *he* doing here?

Another glance confirmed to Asher the man was Heinrich Hammerstill. He owned a gallery that focused on modern art. Last year the man had been featured in an episode of The Art Guys and had made a mockery of Asher before the cameras. Called him just a pretty face and sub-par. The producers had kept that clip in, despite Krew asking them to take it out.

The emotional residue from that experience still clung to Asher's bones. Because in the moment, he'd believed Hammerstill's accusations. Of course he was using his looks to get by. Of course he was lacking in real talent, selling only subpar works and—hell, he didn't even have a stable of artists that he represented. He was merely decoration for the brokerage, the pretty face who attracted clients to the real brokers, Krew and Joss.

Exhaling heavily, Asher winced at the tightening in his chest. He didn't want to believe any of it. Yet now his nemesis was here to remind him that he would never rise above the exterior and gain his own place in the art world.

Did he have competition to see who could get to Tony Kichu first and convince the man to sell his art? It was possible the man knew he was here, but Asher couldn't be sure. Keeping his back to Hammerstill, Asher smiled through his frustration and faked looking interested in Maeve's handiwork. One thing was certain: he needed to up his game and find Kichu. Fast.

"All right, class!" The instructor's voice brought the pottery wheels to a stone-grinding halt. "Looks like you've all created some lovely, if a few slightly crooked, vases. Now for the fun part!"

Asher looked to Maeve, who waggled her brows. She was in a particularly light mood today. Her peach sundress was sashed with a bright pink scarf with black skulls dotting it. It worked on her. A visual cue to her bright and open mood? Tinged with the mysterious skulls. Hmm...

He shouldn't be distracted by German gallery owners, and instead needed to focus entirely on his good fortune to spend time with Maeve, but...he did need to prove to Krew and Joss that he could bring in an artist, not just schmooze at gallery parties and blow up their socials.

"Time for the hugs!" The instructor explained that the couples would stand on either side of the vase and...hug one another, with the vase in between.

"Things just got weird," Asher muttered.

"We do like weird." Maeve gave a tug to the protective vinyl apron she wore, adjusting it to cover the front of her dress. "You ready for this?"

Approving of her jovial reply, he nodded. "I'm in."

With a glance across the room—Hammerstill's back was to him—Asher spread his arms around the vase and leaned toward Maeve. It was going to get messy. But at least this time he wouldn't be forced to perform an intimate act commanded by a shrill whistle.

When Maeve's arms slid along his torso, he did the same with her. Carefully. Testing. The object was to gently press the vase between them, leaving impressions. This was certainly a style of art he'd never experienced. Maeve laughed as her hair dipped across the top of the vase. He brushed it with his fingers then realized they were still covered with clay. And now her hair was. And so was the front of his shirt where the apron didn't cover. Giggles filled the room. Along with a few choice oaths.

"I'm going to need a shower after this," Maeve tittered, "or maybe a dip in the hot springs."

"I'll race you to the springs."

Her eyes twinkled and the apostrophes at the corners of her mouth teased. This was the most awkward yet intense hug he'd been privy to. Cold, squishy clay seeping through his shirt-sleeves didn't dissuade him from enjoying the moment. He didn't want to let go of her warmth, her giddy lightness. Where was that kiss whistle when he needed it?

"I suppose," she said on a whisper, "if we were really a couple in a terrible emotional tangle, I would be feeling a little closer to you right now. Thanks for enduring such a silly class."

"Did I have a choice?"

"Probably not." Her sigh was followed by a smirk, and he sensed she'd taken that the wrong way.

"There's no one else I'd rather hug pottery with than you," he said.

"Yeah?"

"Swear to it. The light…" He tilted his head, allowing more of the light from the nearby window to beam across her face. It glittered on her mouth.

"The light?"

"It always seems to dance with you."

Her glittery mouth formed a surprised O.

"Like that. I appreciate how light changes art." And she was art.

"Everyone part carefully," the instructor called, "and then admire your work!"

Letting go of Maeve was more difficult than forcing himself to start an argument with her. Asher slowly stepped away from the vase, yet found himself snapping to Maeve's side like a magnet. There he felt like he wasn't being judged. Not expected to put on a show and be The Face. He could get messy and squish pottery with her.

"It's brilliant," she said of the crumpled clay. The tall vase was compressed and bent slightly to the left. The impression of Asher's shirt buttons lined one side. And indents from the bow tied in front of Maeve's apron decorated the other side. Along with a few fine lines from her hair strafing the rim.

"I like it."

"And we made it with our own hands." She

nudged his shoulder with hers. "We work well together."

Yes, they did. Asher cast a glance around the room. Most couples were also admiring their work, but one set was arguing over something. Par for the course considering the reason for the getaway. "How are we going to get that thing home with us?"

"Now smash them!" the instructor called.

Maeve gaped at Asher. They'd both fallen in love with something they had created and now… Her jaw closed and a sparkle glinted in her eye. He felt that mischievous glint dance in his chest. With a nod, he confirmed that he knew what she was thinking. They both plunged their fists against the hug-crushed clay and pounded it down to a lump.

After many vigorous punches, they stood back from their destruction. Maeve exhaled. "Now, *that* was good."

Asher lifted his clay-covered fist, and she met him with the obligatory fist bump.

"First one to the room gets the shower." Maeve grinned.

"I'm going to hang back and…" Follow Hammerstill to see what the man was up to. She didn't need to know that he was still bothered by the incident, or that he was worried. "…ask the instructor about her art education. I suspect some Basquiat influence."

"I'll meet you for dinner in an hour."

"It's a date."

She glanced back to him, her chin lifting. The summer light glinted in her irises. In that moment, Asher read her acceptance, and it blasted him with a feeling that lifted him and made him float.

"Yes, a date," she offered, then shyly nodded.

He watched her leave her soiled apron at the door, then walk out. They hadn't gotten the kiss whistle. But he had gotten a sort of hug. And for some reason that meant more to him than all the hugs, kisses and intimate contact he'd gotten from any other woman. Because Maeve wasn't in The Face's life as a prop to use in a social media post. She was just Maeve participating in—

She *was* just faking it for him. How quickly he forgot this week was all play. Was it too much to hope that he might tilt the tables and interest Maeve in seeing him as more than a boss and perhaps even a man who was interested in her?

Did he want that?

You need to get earthy and ugly.

Yes, yes, he did.

CHAPTER NINE

A SELF-GUIDED SOUND experience currently immersed them. Maeve had noted the class, which was about healing sound frequency, and told Asher they should at least give it a try before heading off to their dinner date. It was only twenty minutes. They sat on the patio and closed their eyes, allowing the orchestral music to—do whatever it was supposed to do.

Maeve felt certain she should not allow her mind to wonder, but…really? While she knew this week was a scam, she would be dishonest with herself if she didn't admit to her desire that this fake could become real.

Holding her hand against Asher's heart during yoga and hugging him during that wacky pottery session had gone beyond a friendly touch. She'd felt every molecule of him on her skin. And she couldn't easily brush him off like lint or wet clay. The man was a royal earthy violet in her color index. And violet paired well with the crisp emerald she so often identified with herself.

Dare she push this further and see if he might have a real interest in her?

But how foolish. She worked for the man. And really, a man of his status would never date *the receptionist*. It was beneath him. While Maeve believed everyone was equal in soul and value, it was difficult not to equate riches with status and power. She'd never had dreams of landing a rich man and living the high life. It wasn't in her nature to go after someone because of what he could give her or how comfortable he could make her life. There had to be something inside…

What a crazy session pottery hugging had been. Destruction had never felt so satisfying. And if a girl were to get metaphorical, it could relate to her building her own business, carefully crafting the clay and guiding it into shape—and then standing back as the world smashed it to bits.

Except *she* had done the smashing. And it felt much better to control a failure than to stand back and allow it to happen. Perhaps if she viewed the failed shop as a learning experience instead of the drastically terrible event? But how to do so with her mother's voice sternly reminding her that she had failed? And really, wasn't it time to come to her senses and look for a real job? Not a silly receptionist who was expected to make coffee and appointments. That took little brain power. And it did not offer much potential of moving up the corporate ladder.

Maeve sighed. Ladders scared her. They seemed too unstable. And she much preferred soaring as opposed to climbing.

Smirking at her thoughts, she reminded herself that she'd never been a metaphor girl, and— that session with Asher hadn't been about failure at all. Rather, it had led her farther down the lust path. It was getting harder to convince herself that she must stick to business. Pleasure nudged itself firmly into her being, and along with it came the enticing offering of holding hands, hugging and kissing Asher Dane.

"There's been a twist to our adventure," Asher announced conversationally.

Maeve turned her head to land in his soft stare. She was reminded of *The Awakening of Adonis*. Waterhouse may have been painting *her* clothed in pink satin and leaning over the luscious Adonis reclined amongst the poppies. But in that painting Aphrodite kissed Adonis awake. And that kiss surely hadn't been so quick as the one they'd shared yesterday.

"A twist?" She shook away her fantasies and reached to adjust the volume on her phone so the music played quietly. "More strange than the fact that we are faking being a couple and also faking being at odds?" she whispered.

"I admit, it's difficult to imagine being at odds with you. We can't do the fake fight anymore. Been there, done that."

"I think we solved the *thing* anyway," she said of their fight yesterday. "We'll just have to sulk side by side, give the illusion we're displeased with one another."

"Sulking. It could work."

"But what's this new twist?"

Asher propped an elbow on the patio table. Maeve turned to face him directly. "Remember Hammerstill?"

She ran the odd name over in her thoughts but didn't immediately come to an answer.

"From the television show?" he prompted.

And then she remembered. Heinrich Hammerstill, an art broker to the stars who was also The Art Guys' biggest competition. During season one, episode three, when Asher had still been finding his place after rejoining the company, Hammerstill had won an auction, and afterward, when Asher had gone to shake his hand and offer congratulations, the bullish broker had accused him of having no talent whatsoever. Asher's humiliation had shown on his face, in his curved shoulders and in his softened voice. Krew had tried to get the film crew to cut that segment, but of course, they'd kept that salacious bit. Viewers devoured conflict and drama.

"He's here?" she asked.

Asher nodded. "Noticed him in the pottery class at the back of the room. I think he's with his wife. Maybe. The woman was young. He's an old man. I know he's been married a decade, at least."

"You think he's having an affair? Wait." The real issue stabbed her. "Why is he here? Do you think…?"

"There can be no other reason. He's after Kichu."

"We've still got a chance," she encouraged. "We'll find Kichu before Hammerstill does. Did you speak to him?"

"I had intended to follow him after the pottery class but had a change of heart. I can't believe I didn't notice him until now."

"The classes have been intense and focused. I haven't chatted with anyone besides you."

"Yes, and we have been focused on the fake. After that dressing down, for millions of viewers to see, I'm not up for another encounter. Though…" He exhaled and tilted his head back. "Perhaps I should charge the vanguard, eh? Show him who his competition really is and that I will not be defeated this time?"

"You're very talented and an excellent art broker, Asher. At the time, Hammerstill had the clout. Now? You've surpassed him immeasurably."

He sighed. "Yet I haven't brought in an artist to the brokerage. This is my chance, Maeve. I have to prove myself to the guys. I'm glad we're not filming this."

The idea of their shenanigans being filmed horrified her. "You know I don't like being filmed."

"If you would allow it, you'd gain so many fans. You'd have tons of followers."

"My ego is not stroked by followers and likes. Oh." She winced.

"You think that's what I'm all about?" He sat up and propped his elbows on his knees.

"No, I—"

"I get it. I'm the Face. The one who wins approval and success because of what's on the surface. As Hammerstill clearly stated, there's nothing of substance beneath. And woe to anyone who scratches that surface and sees what spills out."

"It's not like that," Maeve said. Yet she stopped herself from an apology.

He stood and wandered across the threshold into the room, calling back softly, "I'm going to dress for dinner."

Truthfully, Asher did have his egocentric moments.

But he wasn't a man of little substance. He

was a genuine art lover, and the moments when he fell into a painting were the most exquisite. They took her breath away. If she should scratch his surface she would be dazzled by what seeped out. Dare she tell him that? It wouldn't mean anything to him coming from a mere receptionist.

Maeve realized she and Asher had had their first *real* argument.

The fake relationship was going well.

So why did her heart feel as though it had just taken a punch?

Asher leaned his shoulders against the bathroom door. He should not have wandered off like that. How thoughtless of him. Maeve had only stated the truth. A harsh truth. He did get off on an increase in followers and likes. He knew that was terribly egotistic. He'd never been a man to seek attention such as he had over these past few years.

His life had been a series of emergencies and recovery and devotion to his parents. They'd both been very sick, and Asher had spent much of his late teenage years tending to them. He'd been devoted to their care and wouldn't change a thing about it. And then, when he'd gotten away to university and had started his career with the brokerage, his mum and dad had needed him again. He had left The Art Guys because he loved his parents.

Three years ago Avery and Alice Dane had moved to Bath to be near a functional medicine doctor who was dialed into their sickness. He'd treated them with careful attention and knowledge and suggested they move to the country. They'd found a sweet little cottage in a rural area and their health had changed remarkably. And for the first time Asher had felt set loose, free to live his own life. And he'd done so, but at the cost of gobbling any attention he could get and feeding off it. It was something he'd not had those years caring for his parents. He'd always made sure they were the ones who got the attention, because they'd required it.

And now? He had become The Face. When the film studio had told them their new monikers for the show—*Promotion, fellas, it'll grab the viewers!*—Asher had laughed and shrugged and went along with it. He wasn't lacking in self-awareness. Not that he'd ever been vain about his looks. Though, vanity had crept into his veins as he'd begun to capture the attention he'd so desperately needed when playing caregiver to his parents. He'd discerned how to use his looks and charm to get what he desired. And it was useful in his profession. But no one could know it was a mask for the real guy beneath.

Asher Dane loved art. He knew it well. And it moved him. It told him stories, as Maeve had suggested. It spoke to him. It expanded his world beyond his pretty boundaries and invited him in, no expectations required.

The Face, on the other hand, dated beautiful women. Rich women. Models and celebrities. The Face could stand at the center of a party and command attention. The Face was listened to when he talked art. The Face won auctions merely by entering the bid room, wielding a bid paddle and flashing a grin to the competing woman across the aisle. The Face…

Was a sham.

Asher bowed his head. He didn't want to be a stupid moniker to Maeve. For the first time he was feeling a real connection with a woman. This let's-try-new-things-to-make-the-fake-relationship-succeed friendship they'd slipped into could lead to something more. Though, obviously, she looked to him as her boss, a man she'd agreed to help by being his fake girlfriend.

What kind of man asked a woman to do such a thing? How had he thought this was a good idea? He didn't want her to buy into the surface illusion of The Face.

He wanted Maeve to know the man inside.

"Asher?"

He pushed the door open and turned to lean

against the vanity as Maeve looked inside. "Listen, Maeve. I'm sorry."

"There's no need to apologize."

"Yes, there is. I overreacted out there. And I think that was a real fight, not a fake one. It won't happen again. Promise." He gestured toward the main door. "Can we go to the dining room for a nice meal?"

"Of course. We should make a game plan for what to do about Hammerstill."

"No, I mean, to relax. Work is over for the day. I need—" to find himself in her eyes and not as a reflection of The Face "—some quiet conversation. I heard a rumor that Kichu has a gallery on-site. Maybe after a meal we can go find it?"

"Yes, I'd like that."

Asher followed her from the room, and as he did so, he inhaled the ineffable scent of Maeve. It was like a salty spring and fresh summer air. Tinged with the vanilla surprise of an indeterminate something he wanted to learn more about.

Could she see beyond The Face? Dare he let her in? Was he falling into this playacting and beginning to feel, well...*feel*?

CHAPTER TEN

THE DINING ROOM handed guests a picnic basket and suggested they wander outside and enjoy the sunset. Maeve had asked for a blanket, and now they sat at the edge of the forest in a quiet knoll that was manicured for such a scenario. Wildflowers bloomed to either side of them, and the air smelled verdant to match the green and violet sky.

No arguments echoed out from the patio behind the resort, Maeve noted. She wished everyone could have a good, healthy relationship and feel loved. So she'd had a few bad relationships. She'd also experienced good ones. A person had to stay in the game to find their match. She hoped it would happen for her sooner or later, but this weird playacting with Asher tilted her from that hope to fear that he could not see her as anything more than a means to an end. And she wasn't getting any closer to proving to him that she was a valuable asset that deserved a promotion at The Art Guys.

With that discouraging thought she looked across the blanket to where Asher sat with his legs spread out before him, arms crossed, then quickly uncrossed. He hadn't packed suitable reclining clothes, so she granted him the awkwardness he obviously exhibited. He'd foregone a suit coat and had rolled up his white shirtsleeves to below his elbows. His hair was always run-your-fingers-through-it messy but styled. And his glacier eyes looked much warmer with glints of gold twinkling from the candlelight, which flickered from the center of the emptied picnic basket. No color in his wardrobe. On occasion he might go with a pale blue shirt under his gray or black suit. She preferred that shirt. It danced with his eyes. Spoke softly, yet also with a tease she could not ignore.

This evening, she wore her tangerine sundress with a pink and black skull belt. Tangerine always felt slightly anxious yet with a tinge of giddy excitement. She could never decide if the color was happy or urgent. So the belt grounded that conflicting feeling. Yes, skulls were grounding to her. They represented life, in all its stages. Whew! The day had been an interesting one with pottery hugs and an unexpected argument. And it had all left her utterly unsure, to be truthful. About everything.

Thankfully, the food was excellent. They'd

finished an amazing spring pea and asparagus salad. The bottle of wine was almost empty.

"The local wine here is incredible," he said. "Has a deep fruity tone to it that I wouldn't have expected."

"I'm not much of a connoisseur. I drink whatever I can afford."

She sat up straight as the dining room waiter stepped off the path and delivered a plate between the two of them along with smaller plates. A tower of chocolate, cream and fresh blueberries challenged them silently. Asher thanked him as he left with their used plates.

Maeve lifted her fork. "Think we can do this?"

"I'm up for the challenge."

They both forked portions onto their plates, then enjoyed the treat as the solar lamps set around the property suddenly lit up with the darkening sky.

"You're taking in that bright pink in the sky, aren't you?" Asher asked.

"It's mauve. And yes, it's startling. Clear and bright. Like a lingering remnant of a disco party after everyone has gone home. Tired yet exhilarated."

"You do have a way with color. That dress."

She smoothed a hand over her lap, ensuring the napkin was still there. If she dropped food on this fabric it would never come out. "Yes, my dress?"

"It's your color…but…"

"But?"

"I'm not sure. Everything you wear looks great on you, but that color seems a little…tense?"

He'd nailed it. Interesting.

"Tangerine is…apprehensive, I guess you could say. At least, it is to me. I tend to dress emotionally."

"I wonder if you've a bit of color synesthesia?"

She'd never thought about it like that. Synesthesia was a confusion of the senses that some people experienced. They might taste colors or smell shapes. The letters in their alphabets could all be a different color. Sometimes they even heard textures. It was a fascinating thing.

"I surround myself with color as a replacement for…"

For having to step forward and speak out. To put the real, bared Maeve Pemberton out there. Because that Maeve only ever seemed to fail.

"You are an artist who wears her canvas," Asher declared.

Maeve laughed abruptly, then quickly caught herself. "I've never been called an artist."

"I don't see why not. Art is everywhere. It doesn't have to be on a canvas or carved into marble. It's that sky out there that caught your attention. I could see you reading the story of it."

She loved that he'd caught on to her admiration of things in the form of stories. "What's life without a great story? Art is everywhere. We just need to pay attention and let it happen to us."

"Let the story life wants you to have… happen. That's poetic. I see art in this cake," he said with a lift of his fork. Sweet cream dripped to the plate. "The chef gathered ingredients and shaped them into something that others could admire and experience with their senses. And what about that crystal goblet? It's handblown. More artwork."

"Your shoes are art." Maeve joined in on the game. "The pounded leather with the tiny arabesques on the toes was lovingly crafted by a cobbler."

"I do love my Venetian cobbler. Now let's talk about more personal art. Like your eyes." He set down his fork and leaned forward. The flames dancing in his eyes lured her to look at him even as she self-consciously wanted to look away. "You know at one time in history they used to read irises to better one's health?"

"I think some people still do. Iridology?"

"I believe so. Your irises tell a story."

"And what story is that?"

"There's honesty and truth in there but also... something not quite right?"

Maeve set down her fork and pressed her fingers over her mouth as she chewed, looking aside. She'd already confessed to him that she was a failure. Why did he have to state it like that?

"Oh, yes, it's in there. But it's not just your eyes."

Her shyness emerged as he leaned forward more and stared lower.

"Your mouth," he said. "The dark cherry that stains your lips is unexpected, so daring against your pale skin. But the best part of the story is those apostrophes on either side."

"The what?"

"Each side of your mouth, there, indenting your skin like dimples, curls into little apostrophes. Striking," he said on a hush that flickered the candle flame between them.

Falling into his glittering gaze, Maeve melted into the compliments as they formed new images of herself and straightened her spine. She'd never been able to accept compliments without an excuse or an *Oh, it's just...* reaction, but she did not feel compelled to protest this time. Asher's regard held her enchanted.

Or rather, charmed. The Face certainly did know how to work his magic. Whew!

With that realization, she sat back and shook her head. "You're incorrigible."

"What did I do?"

"You've an innate way of enchanting people. When we finally do locate Tony Kichu, deploy that charm so we don't lose him."

"I wasn't deploying anything on you, Maeve." He sat back and rubbed his brow. "Did it feel false?"

No, it hadn't. But this entire trip was all about faking it. How could it have been anything but?

She set her napkin aside. Nothing with Asher felt false. That was what made this all so frustrating. Her body reacted to him as if this were real. Only her brain knew otherwise. "Maybe it's that thing that feels not right, as you mentioned."

She set her plate inside the picnic basket and blew out the candle. The landscape glittered with solar lighting. The mauve in the sky had disappeared. And she suddenly shivered. "It chills so quickly here at night."

"That's why you're feeling not right. Let's head inside."

Maeve stood and handed him the basket. Her phone pinged with a text. She wouldn't normally pay attention to it, but the bright glow from her phone distracted so she tugged it from her pocket and looked at the screen.

"Krew need help?" Asher guessed as he folded the blanket.

"No, it's my mum."

"Anything wrong?"

Her mum had sent a note and a link for a job in Dublin. Marketing intern at a paint company. That was interesting. Also surprising. Her mum wanted her to find a *real* job, but she had never gone so far as to send her a lead like this.

"It's all good. She checks in on occasion." To see if Maeve had come to her senses.

"You said your mum lives in New York?"

"Yes, she's the CEO of LilithTech. Created the business from scratch. But don't ask me to explain it beyond that it's about stocks, investing and focused on helping female clients. She's accomplished so much."

"She must be proud of her daughter."

"What for?" Maeve asked all of a sudden, and then realized her dismissive reaction might not make sense to him. "I mean, well…"

"I'm sorry, I shouldn't have assumed. You've got a fine job at a prestigious brokerage. That must impress her?"

Maeve took the blanket from him and walked up to the pathway, waiting for him to follow. "It takes a lot to impress Mariane Pemberton. A woman who has never had time for anything but moving up the corporate ladder, taking no prisoners and shoving aside any man who gets in her way. I'm not sure that sort of status is something I can or want to achieve. At least, not in the manner my mum expects it to happen."

Asher stepped up beside her. The growing darkness made it necessary to stand close to see one another's faces. Everything felt right about his closeness.

"I get the whole thing about wanting to be whatever your parents expect, Maeve. But don't let it stop you from seeking what your soul desires. I suspect, for you, that's a very colorful desire."

Oh, how he understood her. "Thank you. Sometimes it's nice to hear what I should be telling myself."

He took her hand, and they strolled toward the resort. Asher left the basket and blanket with a staff member, and they wandered inside. A class across the hall from the dining room was finishing. Something about dream reading, if Maeve recalled correctly. The whole rehab week was interspersed with a lot of woo-woo stuff, but she supposed the eclectic mixture was what drew all sorts to Kichu as a relationship coach.

"How about we find that gallery?" He tugged her toward a curving wood staircase, a work of art in itself.

The gallery was tucked above the dining room

on the second floor. Seeing they were the only two in it scurried an effusive joy through Maeve's veins. Enjoying art without the hindrance of a crowd was always the best.

Asher strolled ahead, hands in his trouser pockets, checking out the room's structure. The floor-to-ceiling windows that overlooked the back courtyard and geothermal pools were portioned off with a wall that rose almost as high as the three-story ceiling. To keep daylight from shining across the artwork, obviously. Though now it was dark, and the glow of small spotlights near each painting beckoned.

The first was a Renoir. Asher stopped before it and gave her a glance as if to say "nice," but he didn't speak. His stance told her he was impressed. Head slightly forward, eyes taking in the canvas. Hands in his pockets slipping out and splaying before him as if he wanted to touch but would not. A subtle yearning in that pose. One she knew well.

"If the entire collection is this elegant," he said on a reverent tone, "Kichu's taste alone has me itchy to rep him."

Maeve wandered to the next painting, attracted by the soft colors in the reclined woman's dress. Pre-Raphaelite—Asher's favorite period for painters. She recognized the painting but not the artist. She should know this one!

"Hughes," he said as he shouldered up beside her. This time his glance was more of a lingering summation of her expression. He didn't so much look at her as seem to breathe her in.

Mouth falling open in wonder, Maeve nodded in agreement. Or was it desire? The intimacy between them was growing. They'd gone from office associates who barely knew one another and rarely made contact to walking hand in hand, sharing snippets of their dreams and desires. A stolen kiss. A weird hug.

"Yes," he said on a whisper. "I agree."

Maeve smiled. She didn't even have to ask. He took her hand and they strolled to the next painting. Another from the Romantic era, featuring a besuited man wandering at the edge of a blurry forest, where strange creatures popped out to dance in his wake. Or perhaps to lure him across the thin place he straddled and forever into their clutches?

"The lighting in here is perfect," she said. "Whoever designed this gallery got it right."

"Like candlelight," Asher agreed. "No harsh fluorescents or spotlights. One should always have the pleasure of viewing the masters' works as they had worked on them."

"To consider how light affects paintings I always think of the Sistine Chapel."

"Yes?" He walked around behind her. He

stood so close they were almost touching. Almost. But not quite. Yet he leaned in near enough to nudge her hair with his nose as he asked, "Tell me."

Just a little closer, she thought. *Kiss me there*. On the neck. It would undo her.

Maeve couldn't recall the last time she had been undone by a man. Had she ever? Was it already happening and she didn't label it that because it was so new to her?

"Oh." Maeve caught her wandering thoughts. "Well, I've not been to the Sistine Chapel, but I have read that the natural light is beautiful."

"It is." He winked at her.

Undone was a whisper away…

She cleared her throat. "Yes. Uh…and visitors stand below and admire the frescos that took Michelangelo years to create. At great pains. The man stood on scaffolding and painted, head tilted back." She mimicked the position. "Can you imagine?"

"I certainly hope he had a good chiropractor."

"Right? But what most don't think about is that he had to have needed an artificial light source for when the sun set or the days were cloudy. Candlelight being the only option."

She sighed and felt the warmth of Asher's breath against her neck. "Yes, like that," she decided, of both her story and what was happening right now. "The soft warm light of the candle. So close. Perhaps elevated near to his work. The quiet strokes of the sable brush against the plaster ceiling. The squish of oil paints being placed to form images. He'd perhaps have the Old Testament strewn open nearby. A reference for his work. A random bird may have flown in, perched to nest. And the quiet flicker of the candle flame, illuminating the bold colors he must have had to use for the minimal light."

Asher walked backward, taking her by the hand. "You see art the way I do. You experience the moment paint was laid to canvas. That excites me."

"The painting part?"

"No, the Maeve and her ridiculous obsession with color part." They strolled toward the exit. "What's your favorite scene in the Sistine Chapel? Mine's *The Flood*. I've been fascinated by the animals since I could name them as a child. My mum used to have a big picture book that featured the paintings in the chapel."

"Phemonoe is my favorite," she said. "*The Libyan Sibyl*. I love the exquisite gold-orange-peach gown she wears. The aquamarine table spread. And that book. It's so lush."

"The prophetess in bright robes. Perfect for you."

He understood her obsession with color? This

was…better than undone, this was…a success she'd never realized she needed.

Turning down the hallway that was lined with a wall of windows overlooking the twinkling landscape, the twosome walked hand in hand, but Maeve startled as a whistle blew over the intercom.

"Kiss alert," a voice announced. "You know the drill, people. Set your differences aside and kiss. We're moving toward the halfway mark. You're all doing so well."

When Asher turned and stopped her so her back pressed against the wall, Maeve's heart fluttered. But what he asked next gave her a delicious thrill.

"May I give you a proper kiss?"

"Yes, please," came out breathlessly. Her lungs panted as giddily as her heart.

Asher stroked the hair along her cheek and followed his movement down to her chin, where he glided his fingers along her jaw. Softly. Burnishing his subtle heat into her skin. He then slid a finger over her mouth.

"Art here," he whispered. "A story I want to learn."

Their mouths met. Yellow and mauve burst behind Maeve's closed eyelids, colors so joyous and happy and sensual that her lips curled to a smile as she tasted Asher's kiss. This wasn't a quick peck designed to fulfill some preconceived expectation. This was a kiss. The kiss she had fantasized about since meeting Asher Dane. And it was much more spectacular than any imagined scenario she had concocted.

He was everywhere at once, his earth and rain scent filling her senses. His taste of berries and chocolate melding into deep royal colors. The heat of him stabbed into her aura and connected like two bubbles coalescing. And when he deepened the kiss and she felt her body grow heavy and her knees weaken, his arm swept around behind her and held her firmly against his chest.

Oh, mercy. What was happening?

She was falling. Not to the floor. Not in love. But rather, into the man's story. It wasn't clear or even obvious, but she trod the edges of it, even walked over into the foyer where she felt his strength introduce her to a certain hidden weakness. She accepted and threaded her fingers up through his hair, tugging gently, wanting him always at her mouth. Passionate and needy.

And when he pulled back and caught his breath, she did so as well. He'd stolen her very breath and she didn't need it back. Yet, movement over Asher's shoulder prodded her to focus and—it was Tony Kichu, standing by the window, scrolling on his phone.

In that moment, Maeve's body, still under

Asher's spell, reacted. It was fight or flight. And while logic insisted she stay and fight to keep him close and win another kiss, flight argued that this was the chance they'd been waiting for.

The chance that Asher needed.

She shoved Asher away from her and dashed down the hallway, calling, "You got this!"

"What?" he called after her.

What a silly exit! Maeve hoped she'd done the right thing. She'd left Asher alone in the hallway with the man they'd come to find. Fingers crossed he could charm him.

And then quickly return to her for another kiss.

CHAPTER ELEVEN

WHAT THE HELL? Just when he'd felt it was safe to give Maeve a real kiss—wham!

Asher touched his mouth. She'd shoved him away from their kiss. Had it been so terrible? He hadn't thought so. In the moment, her body had fallen against his. He'd caught her, thinking she might even buckle at the knees. Their mouths had melded, her fingers exploring hair and skin. Her breasts had crushed against his chest. It had been a perfect moment.

"Oh, sorry, didn't see you there."

Asher turned to find a tall, solemn man with long straight black hair standing before the window, a phone in hand. He'd seen a photo of him in the research material Krew had sent him for this trip.

"Mr. Kichu." Asher moved over to shake the man's hand. "It's a pleasure to meet you in person."

Where was Maeve? What she was missing! Had she seen Kichu? Well, he wasn't going to lose this opportunity, despite the nagging inner voice that insisted he'd blown it with Maeve.

"Asher Dane," he offered. "I'm here with, uh…my girlfriend." A would-be girlfriend? Too much to hope for. He wasn't on his game with Maeve. What was he doing wrong?

Kichu was tall and lean, clad in loose white clothing that was probably environmentally, ecologically and whatever else friendly. He wore his hair in a high ponytail that tugged his face smooth. A ski-run nose punctuated his face.

"You are enjoying the experience?" the guru asked in a soft voice tinged with a Japanese inflection.

"It's very interesting. I feel it's…helping. Yes, it's been good for us."

In ways he hadn't expected. Yet had he negated all that good with a kiss? Women did not usually run from him following a kiss.

"I am pleased." The man looked to his phone again. Obviously, not at ease with the conversation. What sort of self-help guru wasn't comfortable with speaking directly to those he sought to help?

No time to wonder. If Asher didn't act quickly…

"I've had opportunity to explore the gallery," Asher said. "I see you enjoy the Romantics."

Kichu nodded, focused on his phone.

"I understand *you* also dabble?"

"Hmm? Yes. Uh…"

"I'd like to see your work," Asher said. "I'm an art broker. My firm represents artists worldwide. We have a stellar—"

Kichu held up a finger. "I have a call I must attend to."

"Of course." Asher strolled about ten feet away from the man, turning his attention out the window as Kichu chatted in another language with someone.

Narrowing his gaze on the solar lamps dotting the back landscape, his heart clenched. Why had she shoved him like that? If she hadn't liked the kiss, she could have politely—well, what?

Maeve baffled him. If it wasn't wondering how to take in her colorful yet boldly clashing exterior, it was turning inward and realizing that he was starting to think she meant more to him than just a receptionist.

When someone beside him said, "Excuse me," Asher stepped aside. An employee pushed a laundry cart past him. After she had passed, Asher turned to Kichu and—the man was gone.

Swearing under his breath, Asher dashed down the hallway to where it met another hall and looked both ways. The man had slipped away without even saying a thing to him? Purposefully? The man was evasive, protecting his privacy at all means. Had he played his hand too quickly? What had happened to The Face's charm?

He hadn't been focused. His thoughts had been split between work and...

"Maeve."

Grass green for her sleepwear. Always. The color made her feel grounded and energetic. All shades of green, but emerald and mint were truly her colors. Maeve brushed her teeth and wandered out to the bedroom just as Asher walked in. With a heavy sigh, he nodded to her and went into the bathroom.

She was eager to learn how it had gone with Tony Kichu, but his sigh did not bode well. Stepping out onto the patio, she tapped both the solar lamps and a soft glow bubbled the two comfy chairs. Glass bottles of water sat on a wood tray, along with a basket of ginger nut biscuits, thanks to the staff who sneakily reset the patios while they were in sessions. She munched a cookie, enjoying the ginger tingle.

Ten minutes later, Asher strolled out in his pajama bottoms and no shirt. Why he did that to her—well, she couldn't request he wear a shirt to protect her eyes from all that fabulous brawn. And really, she enjoyed the view.

"Judging from your sigh when you entered, I'm guessing it did not go well."

He plopped onto the chair, grabbing one of the water bottles. Tilting back a good swallow, he then leaned his head back and took in the vast constellations in the dark sky.

"I did speak to him. But I wasn't on top of my game. He took a phone call, and while I was standing aside, trying to politely not listen, he made his escape. Just vanished."

"What?"

"I didn't get a chance to do more than introduce myself and let him know I was interested in looking at his work."

So he hadn't deployed his charm? Wasn't that The Face's talent? He should have wrapped Kichu around his little finger.

"I was distracted," Asher confessed.

"By what?"

He turned on the chair and set the bottle on the table between them. Lamplight glowed over his face, gifting his skin a golden sheen. Maeve caught a breath at the back of her throat. He was so beautiful. More compelling than any artwork she had seen.

"By the most unique artwork in my world."

His face was sincere and his eyes sought her like an arrow to the target. Struck, she whispered, "What artwork is that?"

"You."

She didn't know how to respond. That arrow detoured from her eyes and soared directly to her heart. He thought she was…? *She* had distracted him?

Well, she had literally just considered how he distracted her.

"But." He leaned back in the chair, his averted attention drawing out the arrow from her chest along with it. "You pushed me away after that kiss. Rejected me."

"No, I—"

"I don't know what I did wrong, Maeve. I did ask your permission."

"Asher." She reached across the table and touched his thigh. "I pushed you away because I saw Tony Kichu. I knew it would be your chance to speak to him. I didn't want you to lose it."

"You could have said something. I was sure you had rejected me."

"There was no time. It was a gut reaction. I didn't want to speak and scare Kichu away. And it worked, yes? You got to introduce yourself to him."

He nodded, but his dreamy stare had resumed. And now he clutched her hand. "I don't care about Kichu right now. I'm glad to learn you weren't shoving me away because my kiss offended you."

"Far from it. In fact…"

Dare she? This was, after all, a fake relationship. Yet they hadn't needed to put on a show for anyone when they'd been alone outside the gallery and the kiss whistle had sounded. Though, it had been a good show for Kichu, obviously.

"In fact?" he prompted.

"It was good that we were kissing when Kichu wandered by, wasn't it? Playing the role of a couple."

"Oh. Of course. We are playing a role. I forgot myself."

"You did?" Was it possible he could have *wanted* to kiss her? She slipped from his grasp.

"Yes. I promise it won't happen again. And when the whistle blows, I will always ask permission." He stood and rubbed at his back. "See you in the morning."

He'd dismissed what she'd hoped was a real connection forming between them. The man was all work and no play. And the way he eased at his lower back with his fingers.

"You can take the bed tonight. That floor is not good for your back, and don't argue about it."

"What if we share? I mean, we've spent the past few nights sleeping in the same room. We know each other well enough... Hell, Maeve, the floor is uncomfortable. And it's only for a few more days. Surely we can share the bed like two adults and not…"

"Oh, of course. Not." Not get close enough to do any of the wild and sexy things she had imagined over and over. "We could…try?"

He nodded. "It's settled then. Which side do you want?"

She followed him into the room, leaving the patio door open, for the night was sultry and warm and there were no insects to worry about fluttering inside.

"Uh…left?"

"Ah, the sinister side. An appropriate choice for my devilishly colorful Marsha."

Smiling at the moniker, she sat on the left side while Asher sat down on the right. He tapped the lamp to darken the room. Moonlight beamed pale luminescence across the bed and his hands. Elegant yet strong hands. Capable of touching her gently. And also commanding her.

Together, they lay on top of the sheets, heads to each of the pillows. While their bodies did not touch, Maeve could feel Asher's body heat waver toward her, tickling its way inside her pores. His royal violet and earthy scent grew heady, the only thing in the room. His presence induced in her a crazy maelstrom of want, desire and caution. If she were to move even slightly, her shoulder or leg would touch his. Would he construe it as an advance on her part? Did she want him to take it that way?

Yes, please. And…

Her mother's voice announced that she would never find her way to success by pleasing a man.

Maeve had no intention of doing such a thing. But how to sort out what was business and what

MICHELE RENAE   145

could become pleasure? Her intention had been
to not allow her heart into this fake relationship.

"This is weird," she finally said.

"Super weird."

She laughed at that agreement.

He added, "We're adults. We can do this."

"Right. We can share a bed. No problem. Just
two business associates away on a work vacation."

"Right. Business associates." His tone sounded
tight. Unsure. Or perhaps nervous, as she was.

Maeve turned onto her side, putting her back
to him. About the only way she could possibly
get through the night. How to sleep with the one
man she lusted over so close to her?

"Just an advance warning," he said. "I'm a
snuggler. It's something that happens when I
sleep. So if you wake up and find my arm around
you, please don't freak out."

Maeve's entire system went into overdrive
when she imagined waking with his arms around
her. "Thanks for the warning. Good night, Windfield."

"Good night, Marsha."

Smiling at their shared joke, Maeve closed
her eyes and knew the only way she was going
to sleep tonight was if the sandman poured out
his entire sack.

CHAPTER TWELVE

MAEVE'S COLOR CHOICE this morning was certainly interesting. Asher took in her violet-striped chinos, the bright yellow T-shirt and the dash of brick-red scarf around her neck. It was a good thing he was attracted to her or he'd have to wear sunglasses to be in the same room.

Fortunately, they were outdoors, surrounded by lush forest and the chitter of insects. A strange bird call fascinated him; he had no clue what kind of bird it belonged to. Captivated by the light pouring through the tree canopy, and also distracted by Maeve's colors, he had to caution himself to keep one eye on the trail.

Maeve walked ahead on the unpaved hiking trail formed by smoothed earth and the occasional stone or log embedded in the path. She paused often to inspect an interesting plant or mushroom. Today's assignment was a hike. They had been emailed a list of questions to discuss at various spots along the trail.

He was thankful he'd brought along a pair of

running shoes because the terrain was rough. And after deciding a white dress shirt wouldn't quite go with the knee-length shorts he'd packed, he'd made a trip to the gift shop and now wore a heather T-shirt with a rainbow-colored logo depicting a circle and clasped hands. It still smelled of the lavender incense that had been burning in the shop. He may have beat Maeve on the weird clothing scale today.

The things he did for his job.

But smelly fashion aside, the day was cloudy yet warm, and the forest they trampled through smelled amazingly verdant and wild, and even a little musty. None of the sensory information was processed too intensely because it had to compete with his thoughts about Maeve.

He had woken this morning with an arm draped over her waist. Still sleeping, she hadn't been aware of his closeness. He'd lingered, taking in her warmth. He could have snuggled closer, buried his face in her hair to inhale her vanilla scent, but he'd caught himself. He wasn't a creep. Though he had closed his eyes and… breathed her in.

Then he'd carefully slid away his arm and sneaked out of bed, leaving Sleeping Beauty to wake on her own. He'd brought back pastries while she had showered.

Whatever was happening between the two of

them, it involved a push and pull. He still wasn't sure if she was going along with the fake or if she saw him as something more than a boss who needed her help. It had only been a few days. He mustn't expect her to fall madly in love with him.

But the thought that she may put a smile on his face. He and Maeve Pemberton? What a unique pair. It was like hanging a Michelangelo beside a Pollock. The two didn't go together at all. And yet, they did warrant attention.

"There's a rest stop ahead," Maeve called over her shoulder. "Did you bring along water?"

"And two pastries."

"You are an excellent packer," she declared as she set aside her hiking pole and leaned on a wood railing that overlooked a narrow creek. "It's so beautiful out here!"

Yes, she was. Er, right. She was talking about nature. Eh. Same thing.

"Does an excellent packer forget to bring along casual wear?" He handed her a bottle of water from the backpack the resort had issued them. "Pastry?"

"Not yet. You couldn't have known this retreat would require all this outdoor exercise and yoga and such. I like the purple shirt on you. It's a tint of your real color."

"My real color?"

"Yes, your scent is like a royal violet, mixed with rain and earth. I see you as that violet color. Like something a king would wear, only a little dusty around the edges."

"I've never been described in such a manner. Usually the media leads with cocky, charming and self-important."

"You believe everything the media writes, don't you? I mean, it is all true."

He cast her a surprised gape and playfully punched her upper arm. "Thanks a lot, Marsha."

"Don't worry. I know the arrogant charm is a facade."

"Do you? Because some days I'm not sure myself who Asher Dane really is."

"There's a kind and caring man under The Face," she said. And then she dared to add, "The Face is a bit of a fake, like we are this week."

"Maybe." He leaned forward on his elbows and peered down over the bubbling creek. She was spot-on. "The Face does get The Art Guys the media buzz required to be a success."

"I can understand the need to hold your own alongside Joss and Krew. You three are remarkable."

"If you say so." If he was so remarkable, then why didn't he have a stable of artists like the other guys? "This has been an interesting few days. I thought it would be a bunch of dull classes inside an auditorium."

"Same."

"So what's the question for this stop?"

She pulled out her cell phone and scrolled. "Hmm, we tell each other what we want for our future. An easy one. I've already told you I have plans to someday own a color consulting business."

"And I hope that dream becomes your reality. My future?"

He turned to rest his elbows on the railing and studied her face. Those long black lashes looked as though they had mascara on them, but he knew she wore little to no makeup beyond the deep red lip stain. A heady tease to his libido. And after waking beside her this morning? His future suddenly seemed so unimportant.

And yet... "Beyond wanting to win over Kichu and prove to the guys I'm the entire package. As well, I've been feeling the call to become...less."

"Less?"

"Yes, less...The Face. More real. Not so out there. Honestly? Maeve, I want to start a family. To know what love is like and to share that with another person."

"Doesn't everyone?"

He glanced to her. "You want a family?"

"Oh, yes, it's an important part of life. Learning to share and love and teach."

"Yes, teach." His kids would appreciate the arts, but they would develop their own likes and dislikes independent of their parents' desires. "And limits on the social media stuff for the kids," he added.

"You don't want your children to have as many followers as you do?"

"That's The Face, Maeve. Not me."

She compressed her mouth and the apostrophes deepened. He reached to touch one of them, which startled her.

"Sorry." He shrugged. "Those apostrophes are so cute."

She touched the edge of her mouth.

He'd stymied her. But he liked seeing her undone. A little off. An unsteady flicker brightened her green eyes. How the light did love her. There was never a moment Maeve Pemberton's light did not attract him.

"The Face was created by the show producers," she stated.

"You get it."

"I do." She tucked her phone away and leaned against the railing beside him. "Why did you leave The Art Guys for those few years? You mentioned something about your parents? I know you also said it was personal…"

Asher crossed his arms, leaning against the railing. It was personal, but Maeve had inserted herself into that private space, and he wanted her to know she was safe there. As he felt safe telling her about it.

"My parents have been sick for a good part of my life. It started when I was a teen. None of the many dozens of GPs they saw could determine why. They prescribed medications that never worked. Some even seemed to make them worse. One time my mother had a severe reaction to a medication that saw her in hospital for weeks."

"I'm so sorry. What is it they have? And both the same thing?"

"We didn't learn what it was until a few months before I returned to the brokerage. They suffered malaise and dizziness and general fatigue. So much so that some days they could barely walk. They needed me to get groceries and cook meals for them most days. General household upkeep was my job, as well as taking care of the lawn. And forget about them being able to drive. I would take them to the GP. Caring for them occupied my teenage years. I was able to go to university and start the brokerage, but it became apparent they needed full-time care, so that's why I left for those years."

"Asher, I'm so sorry. That must have been difficult for you growing up. Did you have friends?"

"Not many who would understand I couldn't
go to the cinema because I needed to watch my
parents. And dating was a bust. Well, I did take
out a few girls. But I could never get beyond
worrying about my parents to really enjoy myself. It wasn't until I was on a flight headed to
an auction and read an article online that I began
to piece things together.

"A massive cell phone tower had been in-
stalled very near where we lived months before
my parents began to show symptoms. It was possible they had developed EMF sickness."

"I've heard of that. Some people can't endure
the radiation and frequencies put out by electronics like mobile phones and Wi-Fi."

Wow, she understood! He didn't have to face
off against disbelief or accusations that it was
all in his head. Something that occurred all the
time as he'd been navigating his parents' sickness with them. Such experience had formed
a hardened shell on his exterior. Perhaps even
had planted the seeds to The Face. Given him a
mask to wear to fend off those who thought he
was ridiculous.

"Exactly, and sometimes even the electricity
wiring a home," he continued. "Our lives are
flooded with electromagnetic frequencies that

are not aligned with our body's natural frequencies. We are electrical beings. We're not meant to swim in a literal electronic soup. It's a difficult diagnosis and most doctors dismiss it as all in the patient's head."

"But you weren't affected by it?"

"Not everyone will be affected as severely as my parents. Though I do take precautions. I don't carry my phone unless it's necessary. Keep it on airplane mode whenever possible. And most of my suit coat pockets are lined with a faraday fabric that blocks electromagnetic frequencies, keeping the radiation away from my body. It's also why you can never contact me in the middle of the day. I don't turn my phone on unless I need it. And have you ever seen me use a laptop or tablet? I don't, unless it's a client's and I need to show them something."

"I'm glad you explained that to me. I would have never guessed. And your parents? How are they doing now?"

"All my research led me to a GP who knew exactly what the issue was. He suggested mum and dad relocate to the country, get as far from London and the digital world as possible. Which wasn't an easy task. Eventually they found a place just outside Bath. An old cottage that was still wired from the early nineteen hundreds and used bells and rope to signal the staff and has a chicken roost outside and—well, it does have modern plumbing. It's the perfect home for them. And they've improved ninety percent."

"That's so good to hear. And that's when you were able to return to the brokerage?"

"Absolutely. My parents have always harbored tremendous guilt over my having to care for them. I could have hired in-home care, but believe me, I would have never wanted to be anywhere else."

"I'm so glad they found a place to live that allows them to be healthy. You are a good son."

"I can't imagine treating them any differently than they treat me. I'm blessed to have been raised in a loving family." And to have found a woman who truly seemed to understand him. Remarkable.

"So that makes me curious about how The Face works into all this?"

"What do you mean?"

"How should I put this without offending you…?"

Asher crossed his arms over his chest, sensing what was coming. "Go for it, Marsha."

She smirked. "The Face is charismatic and charming. Out there. He knows how to work a room *and* a person to get what he wants. Doesn't really jive with the kindhearted son who sacrificed years of his work at The Art Guys to care for his parents."

She got him. She really got him.

"I think The Face burst out of me following that stint caring for them. Part of me..." He winced. He'd thought about this after that class on emotions. And it was so true it hurt. "I craved the attention. And I saw what a charming smile and some complimentary words could do to a person as I was navigating the health care system with my parents. I learned I could get through any situation with body language and, yes, even some manipulative words. I'm not proud of it, but I quickly learned that one must have an advocate, a voice, when they are struggling through the health care system. I had that voice. And I softened it and gave it a flirtatious tone because it got me to where I needed to land."

"I can understand that. Please don't feel guilty. You did what you had to do for your parents. You gave your life to them, sacrificing a social life and friendships. It makes sense you'd want to grab it all now."

"Just because it makes sense doesn't mean it's right. That arrogant charm you mentioned has outgrown its stay. I don't like that label. I mean, I work it. I know what The Face brings to the brokerage. Sure, I'll take the credit for bringing in the media interest. But I'm so glad you can see the real me."

"I have always seen that man." She collected her water bottle and stood to turn toward the path. "And I like what I see."

She marched onward, into the sweet piney forest. And Asher's heart followed before his footsteps did.

"She likes me," he whispered. And it felt as wondrous and exciting as if a younger version of himself had discovered love for the first time.

Later Maeve munched a chocolate macaron as she wandered along the rocks edging the same stream they'd crossed earlier. She sat on a large rock, kicked off her shoes and dipped her bare feet in the water. So nice after walking for hours.

They'd discussed a few more questions.

Reveal something you've never told your partner.

She had kept it light by telling him she was afraid of the color puce. *Come on! Who names a color that?* And he'd played along to reveal he couldn't brush his teeth without mentally singing "Twinkle, Twinkle Little Star."

A few deeper questions remained on her list. But she was enjoying herself too much to wander into those. The day was perfect. And with no one else but Asher beside her, she could relax.

Forget about making the future a success. Leave her mother's chastising words in a dark corner. Be in the present.

Settling beside her, Asher peeled off his socks and plunged his feet into the water. "Cold!" He cringed, but then placed his feet back in the water. "But invigorating. A nice pick-me-up after hiking for so long, eh?"

His wink hit her right where all that soft mushy swoony stuff had been collecting over the years. Right now, a kiss would make that stuff explode from her like a volcano spewing lava. Probably best to contain herself. Or maybe not? They were alone…

"I think the resort is beyond that thick of trees," she said.

Asher reached for her mouth. "May I? You've macaron crumbs…"

"Oh. Uh…sure."

He wiped off the crumbs. Taking his time. Eyes focusing intently on her mouth. And if that wasn't an invitation…

Maeve leaned forward and pressed her lips to his. Kissing Asher was a dream come true. They were having some fun learning about one another. And the bonus was the growing intimacy.

His fingers threaded through her hair at her nape, tickling an erotic shiver along her spine. Leaning into him, she deepened the kiss. This was a moment she would never forget. And yet, she did work for him, and—how would Krew and Joss take this?

Breaking the kiss and touching her lips, she whispered, "I shouldn't have done that."

"Why is that?"

"Asher, you're my boss."

"Believe me, Maeve, when we kiss it has nothing to do with the fake relationship. Well, that first one in the yoga class might have been. But since then? I kiss you because I want to. And you kissing me?"

"I couldn't not kiss you," she hastily confessed. "And...I don't want it to be fake, yet..."

"Yet?"

"I don't know. It doesn't feel right, no matter how often I think about—"

She caught herself. Tugged in her lower lip with her teeth. How often she thought about kissing him? How *not* winning him would only notch another failure for her tally?

"Please don't let me being your boss bother you," he said with a quick kiss to seal that statement. The way he looked at her always stole her breath. As though there was no one else in this world. She was his focus. "There are no rules saying we have to keep it business only."

"Sounds good. In theory. But what about when the week is over and the goal is accomplished?

Do I return to my desk, leery of making eye contact with you and regretful that this, whatever it is, didn't become something more?"

"Do you…want something more?"

"You see? You think this is just for the week. And when we return to London it's back to the status quo again. I can't risk the heartache."

"But that's what life is for, Maeve. You're supposed to let it happen. I promise I won't ghost you."

She stood, grabbed her shoes and stepped up the mossy bank to the hiking trail. "I don't know. This feels…suddenly dangerous." Stuffing her wet feet into her running shoes, she twisted until they slid in. "I should have never said anything. Should have played along with the fake relationship. But it's never been fake to me. I…need to be alone for a bit. Give me a five-minute head start."

She dashed off, double-time.

She felt like a fool. The kiss had been perfect. Yet she had allowed a ridiculous misgiving to nudge into that perfection. She'd failed. But not in a manner her mother would scoff at. Mariane Pemberton would approve of Maeve avoiding utilizing a man on her climb to the top.

If she pleased her mum, then ultimately Maeve felt she would never win. At least not when it came to her heart.

CHAPTER THIRTEEN

ASHER FOLLOWED MAEVE'S retreat until she turned toward a curved trail amongst the trees.

It's never been fake to me.

Really? She'd *always* had feelings for him? That was remarkable to learn. And it wasn't as shocking as he expected. Because he may have felt the same only never realized it. Until this trip.

Until he'd kissed the girl and she'd run away. Again.

He took a different path around back of the shower building toward the far end of the resort. He wasn't sure if that door would open from the outside. He and Maeve hadn't yet ventured that way. Worth a try.

Walking up the wood-paved aisle toward the door, he spied a man coming out from the building and his mood rose in anticipation—until he saw who it was.

"Hammerstill," he muttered tightly.

The gruff representation of a living tree stump

recognized him and shook his head. "If it isn't The Face. My partner thought she saw you here, but I couldn't imagine a man like you being in a relationship long enough to have trouble."

"Same," Asher said. "I thought you were married, Hammerstill? And not to the woman I've seen you here with. Got a little something on the side going on?"

The man winced. Asher had guessed correctly.

"None of your concern."

"You're right. Your private life isn't of interest to me. What is, is that you seem to be here for ulterior motives. Not necessarily interested in rehabbing whatever it is you're tagging as a relationship?"

"I could imagine the same of you. You after Kichu?"

"Maybe. Spoke to him last night, in fact."

"Is that so?" The man crossed beefy arms over his barrel chest. "How did that go? Wait. Let me guess. You charmed him with your million-dollar smile and dazzled with that easy camaraderie. And then when it came time to seal the deal? You choked."

The bastard was so presumptuous! Asher didn't choke. He'd never lost a client or failed to obtain the best deal and art those clients expected of him. One time—unfortunately, on film—he'd lost an auction. And that thought switched his brain to Maeve telling him how her mother told her she was a failure. He knew exactly how Maeve felt!

"You choked again, Dane?" Hammerstill prompted.

"Kichu had a meeting." Asher set aside his thought about Maeve. "We plan to talk. Soon."

"We'll see about that." Hammerstill lifted his burly chest and pointed in the air defiantly. "The race is on!"

He barged past Asher and made his way toward the geothermal pools.

Yes, the race was on. And Asher had a leg up because he'd already made contact with the elusive artist. Now to get a look at the artwork everyone wanted to own.

He tried the door and found it locked. Exit only? Figures. Tracking along the building so Hammerstill didn't notice his defeat, he rounded the resort and veered toward the reception area. But the thought of Maeve failing in her mother's eyes bothered him.

She needed support. He knew that feeling.

Maeve had managed to avoid Asher for a few hours by slipping into a "girls only" session on Making Time for Yourself. The trouble was, she had too much time to herself. And she wasn't in a real relationship. The class information had wafted around her ears, slipping in and out while her thoughts were preoccupied with the tiff she and Asher had earlier. For a pair who were not even a couple in real life, they seemed to be meeting plenty of challenges. The fake relationship had become reality.

And that confused the bloody heck out of her.

The class ended, and Maeve slipped out with a quick "thanks" to the instructor. It was evening, and hunger nudged her stomach, so she headed toward the dining room.

It hadn't been a tiff. Well. She had allowed herself to admit to him that she wished what was going on between them might be more. But she knew it wasn't to him. Those kisses? He was playing a role.

Or maybe he wasn't?

Again, the confusion would end her. What was real and what was fake?

She, unfortunately, had *not* been role-playing. It was impossible not to allow her heart into the act when the man she desired touched her and kissed her and had slept beside her all night. She'd woken in the pale morning hours to feel Asher's arm draped across her waist. It was as if her body wanted her to be alert, to note the touch, so she'd woken in a sort of reverie.

His arm across her waist had been an unconscious act. But for those minutes when she'd lain there like a statue, because she hadn't wanted to wake him and lose the touch, she had experienced some heady emotions. Romance and passion. Excitement and desire. Bliss, comfort, even satisfaction. As if they were a real couple and it had been just another morning wrapped in one another's arms.

Then she had cautioned her fantasies. Everything she knew about Asher Dane was being turned on its head. He wasn't an egotistic spotlight seeker. His need for attention had been a result of years of selfless attention to his sick parents. He deserved the notice he got now!

She wanted to reach into him and make him understand that she cared about him. That she was on his side.

It felt risky. And premature. And yet, he had indicated that his kisses were because he *wanted* to kiss her and not in a fake way—but for real.

Her phone pinged and she tugged it from her dress pocket. While stalking back to the resort from the hiking trail, she'd opened the link to the application her mum had sent for the Dublin job. In that moment she'd felt, at the very least, she should apply and see what the job might offer her. A backup may be wise should her prospects with The Art Guys fall flat. The text confirmed her application had been received. They would notify her soon if they wished to set up a video interview.

"It's being smart," she said to her unsure thoughts. "I have to keep my options open."

Especially since she wasn't expecting this trip to advance her at The Art Guys anymore. All she was learning from Asher was how to sneak around.

Entering the dining room, she immediately saw Asher at the back near the window. He gestured her over. A good sign he wasn't angry with her. Not that he should be. Hell, *she'd* stormed away from *him*. She was not a drama queen. Yet she'd not been prepared for the roller coaster of emotions soaring through her this week!

"I wasn't sure you'd come," he said as she seated herself across the small table from him. Candlelight glinted in his hair and pale irises. "Bold red and a dusty turquoise," he said of the colors she'd chosen with great care before heading off to the Making Time for Yourself class. "What does that mean?"

To Maeve, red meant putting up a shield to keep others back. She'd been apprehensive while dressing. Now she felt more like the blue scarf that indicated a cool yet cautious eagerness.

"Just a dress I pulled out from the closet." She picked up the goblet and sniffed the deep red wine. "Fruity."

"It's delicious. But I don't for one moment believe that you just threw on that dress."

She quirked a brow. "You think I'm lying?"

"I would never accuse, but…" He nodded while he shrugged.

Caught. "Doesn't matter what it means. What's for dinner?"

"Four courses. Filet mignon. Tiny potatoes. Fussy foamy stuff. You know the deal. I suspect that red…"

He wasn't going to let it go!

"Is…" He rolled his thoughts over so long she could see the process dance in his eyes. "It means stop," he decided.

Maeve couldn't prevent a chuckle. "That's a no-brainer. But no."

"No?"

"I'm not so obvious with my colors." She decided to throw him a bone. "It's caution. Maybe a bit of exterior armor. I feel like we went the wrong way out on the hiking trail. Or I did. I shouldn't have said the things I did."

"About wanting this to be more?"

Wow, he grabbed right for the arrow lodged firmly in her heart. Maeve nodded, thankful when the waiter arrived with their plates, which featured a miniscule chunk of what she hoped was red meat surrounded by pink drizzle and some truly Lilliputian carrots, with the greens barely fraying to the plate edge.

"This is one bite for me," Asher said.

"I hope the dessert is an entire pie." Maeve lifted her fork. "Thank goodness for the monster pastries they serve at breakfast."

"When this is over I promise to take you out and treat you to a real meal." He lifted his goblet to toast and Maeve met it in a *ting*. "We both need real food."

"Hear! Hear!"

"For every tiny carrot you eat," he suddenly said, pausing her with a fork tine speared with a marble-sized carrot, "I want some truth."

Maeve lowered her fork. "About what?"

"Do you really want this to be a thing? Us?"

She stared at the carrot, pearled with butter sauce. If she didn't confess her truth they would leave and go back to the same old, same old. She may or may not earn a raise or chance to prove herself worthy of a promotion. It was what she desired.

And yet. Advancement was only a step toward her goal. She wasn't going to erase her mother's voice from her brain after a few days at a couples' spa. So why not reach for something that she desired in equal amounts? Like the handsome man waiting for her to speak.

Maeve ate the carrot. One chew. Time for the truth.

"I do," she finally said.

Asher nodded appreciatively and tilted back a long swallow that emptied his glass. He signaled to the waiter, who brought over another bottle and refilled his.

"I know it's silly," Maeve started.

"I certainly hope not," he said defensively. "Else I might think you're playing another kind of game. And I'm not sure how to play that one."

"You see?" She set her napkin on the table and sat back, feeling frustration swell and chase away her appetite. "That's the problem. We're playing games. *Are* they a couple? *Are* they having trouble? Can they sleuth out the elusive artist? Will they win him over? Can she earn a raise? Can she ever fulfill her dream?"

Asher reached across the table and placed his hand over hers. He nudged her, and she turned her hand up so he could clasp it properly. "I could make that dream of yours come true right now. How much do you need to open the consulting business?"

Maeve slid quickly from his grasp. "I don't want your charity."

"I know. And though it was a genuine offer, please don't think I was trying to buy you for— I know you need to do this on your own. That's what makes a dream a dream. It's something a person accomplishes. It isn't handed to them."

Maeve felt a tear threaten in her eye. He understood.

"I ran into Hammerstill earlier," he said. "He's my nemesis. Makes me feel like… You saw the footage. And he made me think about what you said about your mother calling you a failure. You are not a failure. You are one of the most put-together, smart, amazing women I know. You'll have another chance at that shop. I know you will."

That tear was almost ready to spill…

"I care about you, Maeve."

He pulled her hand up and kissed it.

"Thank you. That means a lot. You're not a failure either. Hammerstill is a bloody pompous jerk who saw an opportunity to bring someone down to his level and jumped at it. You shouldn't let it continue to bother you."

"I thought I was the one encouraging you? You're so caring toward others. That's not being a failure. That's a special quality not many possess."

"You're the same. After hearing about how you cared for your parents for years? Asher, you are a strong man. You don't need to prove yourself to anyone."

"That said, I do genuinely want to develop my own stable of artists."

"This could be your chance. It will happen."

She sipped her wine and her shoulders relaxed.

"Now back to the real topic of conversation." He laid his palms on the table before him and met her gaze. "I'm not sure what is happening between us right now, but I don't want to run away from it. And I don't want it to be a game we're playing. We're mixing business with pleasure here. And while that has sometimes been a norm for me, it feels off. Just as you said. This is…different. And you deserve more attention than I can offer when I should be focused on the goal."

She didn't like hearing what he seemed to not want to clearly state. That he had to focus on work. And she was a distraction. Never had she felt like a distraction to a man. And truthfully? It was more exciting than it should be. Especially since she knew the one rule of this game: it's all fake.

"We are workmates," she stated to remind herself. "Not something we should risk destroying because of some silly game we decided might win us an artist."

"Maeve, the whole boss/employee thing doesn't bother me. That shouldn't affect our work in any manner. You make me feel…" He searched his thoughts. "*Feel*, Maeve. Things I haven't felt be-

fore. It's like I don't have to work for your interest. The Face means nothing to you. You give
me your attention freely. That means so much.
And I don't want to stop kissing you. And I don't
want to stop waking in the morning with my arm
draped across your body."

So he'd known they had touched, slept so
close? And he'd not said anything. Kept it to
himself. As she had chosen to do the same. A
silent passion. Of course she'd given him her
attention freely. It wasn't difficult. But keeping
it was the challenge. One that they both needed
to face.

"But I do need to catch the client before Hammerstill does," he said. "And so…"

"I understand. I do."

"I don't think you do understand how much…"

The waiter arrived to take away their plates.
A few bites had not satisfied Maeve. How could
she eat when her relationship was the topic?
They both wanted to go that direction. There
was only the distraction of still playing the fake
in the way.

She didn't understand how much *what*? He
cared about her?

Another waiter arrived with dessert, sweeping
it grandly before them before placing it precisely
at the table center. It wasn't miniscule. It was a
tower of vanilla cake smothered in red sauce and

fresh cut fruit, served on a massive plate with two dainty forks placed to either side. This place was certainly focused on satisfaction via sweets!

As her gaze met Asher's wide eyes, the two of them laughed at the silliness of the meal. And it released some of the tension she felt over what was happening between them. He'd kind of, sort of confirmed he might feel the same about her. But he didn't want to focus on her right now.

Of course, this was a business trip. And she was determined to make advances, no matter how little they may ultimately serve her goal. Time to get her head back in work mode.

CHAPTER FOURTEEN

THE EVENING WORKSHOP was in the gymnasium. The couples sat on yoga mats but were promised they wouldn't be flexing any body parts tonight. Candles flickering everywhere gave the room the aura of a cathedral, one of peace and safety.

Maeve noticed the couples who had been arguing most virulently at the beginning of the retreat had seemed to settle, sat a bit closer, some even held hands.

The instructor thanked them for their participation in the hike that one couple had gotten lost on. They'd had to send in a rescue team to find them; they were recovering in their room this evening.

"Those questions we sent along with you weren't that difficult, were they?" the instructor joked. "Sorry. We have one final question that requires your discussion this evening. And that is, now that you've shared your dreams and goals for the future, how will your partner help you to achieve that goal? Okay? Discuss!"

Asher's shoulder hugged against hers, and he leaned in to whisper, "We've got this one, Marsha."

"Do we?" While comfortable snuggling against him, she wasn't as confident as some of the couples who had found new reason to reconnect with their partners. Asher wasn't her partner. Much as she wanted him to be. "I can't help you with your goal."

"Wrong. You are helping me. You were the one who ditched my kiss so I'd have the opportunity to talk to Kichu. It was my fault I failed the task."

"Don't call yourself a failure."

"Oh, yeah? I won't if you don't."

"But I am…"

He slid his hand into hers and tilted his head against hers. "Maeve, not many women succeed in opening a shop in a large city at such a young age. You are remarkable. You had a vision. You fulfilled it. It wasn't your fault some nasty virus decided it wasn't time for something so innovative as a color shop."

"I've never thought of it that way."

"You should. You succeeded. Now you'll try again. And you will accomplish your goal."

"But I don't see you having a hand in that. I don't need anyone's help."

He bowed to meet her gaze. "It's okay to ask

for help. Support. And I'm not talking financially. I want to be there for you."

A warmth swirled in her chest. The words felt like kindness come to color in soft violet. "Why?"

"Because you matter to me. I care about you."

Hearing him relabel her failure as something akin to an accomplishment twisted all the beliefs her mother had implanted in her over the years and forced them to the surface.

"I'm not sure I can succeed again," she said softly. "I got a loan from my mum the first time. I won't ask her again."

"Then you'll go to a bank. You'll bring along the best references from me, and I'm sure Krew and Joss will offer theirs as well."

"That's very kind of you."

"I'm not offering to bankroll your project because I understand that you like to do things on your own. But know, the offer still stands."

"I appreciate that, and...I won't forget."

"Hey, you file all my tax forms and banking information. You know what I make. I can afford to support a woman-owned color therapy business."

Maeve laughed softly. "I have seen your bank statement. It's obscene. But..."

"But?"

"It's not who you are. You are not defined by

your bank account or by what your millions of followers think of you. I know that. But do you know that?"

"I thought we were talking about you?"

"You have a tendency to deflect the topic of conversation when it veers toward you."

"Guilty. Fine. I believe my worth is not based on the opinions of others. But The Face does love to play the game."

"The Face is a part of you that you should never abandon. But don't you realize it's not about The Face? You need to let the real Asher Dane out more often. I like him."

"You like me?" He nudged her playfully with his shoulder and sing-songed, "Marsha likes me."

"There's a lot to like."

"Now you're being sappy." He touched the corner of her mouth. An apostrophe? She'd always thought those crinkles were superfluous and annoying, but when he touched them, she was thankful for her uniqueness.

"Class," the instructor called, "your homework for tonight will be intense."

Gazes darted around the room. Maeve straightened next to Asher, who winked at her. Intense for a fake couple pretending to fight who had decided in real life to chill everything? But then again, maybe not? Could her life be more confusing right now?

"That mirror in your room is there for a purpose," the instructor announced.

Maeve's heart dropped. She could feel Asher's body tense beside her.

"Tonight you'll sit or stand before the mirror, fully clothed, and touch one another. Really feel your partner's very being. Go inward and see how that makes you feel. Can you connect on a level beyond sex? You can give instructions where you are comfortable being touched. Touch but no sex! All right, good night, everyone. See you all in the morning."

Asher stood and held out his hand to Maeve as she rose beside him. "I think that red you're wearing fits the moment," he said. "Caution."

He hit that one right on the mark.

Maeve stood before the mirror studying the wrinkle in her tomato-red dress. The fabric never stayed smooth. But she wasn't an ironing kind of girl. For some reason, staring at the wrinkle distracted her from looking at the woman standing before a floor-to-ceiling mirror anticipating what must come next.

Asher was in the bathroom brushing his teeth. They'd laughed as they'd returned to the room, suggesting they try the mirror assignment. Just for kicks.

Just for kicks. And the highest stress level she

may have ever registered. Because she wanted Asher to touch her. Everywhere. But not because someone assigned them to do so.

"Why are you doing this to yourself?" she whispered.

"What was that?"

The scent of mint preceded Asher as he swung around the corner and into the main room.

His reflection showed freshly tousled hair.

That she could lose herself in.

A charming smile.

That she could surrender to.

Crisp business shirt unbuttoned two buttons down.

That she wanted to remove.

And a curious tilt of his head as he discerned her inner thoughts.

Maeve caught herself and checked her stance. No drool. No leaning toward the man she wanted to inhale, devour and consume. "Wondering if this assignment is too silly to attempt?"

"Nonsense." He stepped up behind her, and placing his hands on her shoulders as if a gentle teacher set to guide her, he smiled at her in the mirror. "It'll be interesting. That is…are you okay with me touching you? I'm okay with you touching me."

"Oh, yes," she said, a little too quickly. "I mean, we've kissed. We are…"

He leaned closer and said near her ear, "We've started something, Maeve."

Oh, yes, they had.

"And this assignment isn't so much about the touch as the connection. At least, that's how I understand it."

True. Which promised to be much more intense. If they did it correctly.

"Can I—" he stepped closer so she could feel his chest against her back "—hold your hands?"

She nodded.

He clasped her hands from behind, and the move pressed him even closer to her backside. They weren't body to body, but their distance would not allow the sneakiest of warm summer breezes to slip between them. Thinking of which, she'd opened the patio doors to allow in the night air. Somewhere in the background a bird cooed, perhaps luring his or her mate to snuggle for the evening.

"Remember," he said on a teasing tone, "no sex…"

Maeve let out a nervous chitter. "Of course not. That would be breaking the rules."

But not her rules. Not in a million years would she ever push away Asher Dane and refuse to make love with him. She wanted him. And… was this too dangerous a task to attempt? To allow him to touch her. To touch him. And to *not* have sex?

"Certainly, we must have our rules," he whispered.

She glanced at his reflection in the mirror and spied his smirk. What was she getting into?

"I understand what this assignment is supposed to do," he said. His fingers loosened within hers, and his hands began a slow glide to her wrists and up her bare arms.

"What's that?" she asked as calmly as possible. Her skin began to electrify and her body to sing. He paused at her elbows, and the soft trace of his fingertips along the insides of them insisted she close her eyes to keep from looking into his delving gaze.

"It's a trust thing," he said. "But also, how many couples really touch?"

"I think that's a thing when you're a couple," she said. "I mean, you can't be one and not touch."

"Sure, but hear me out." He glided his fingertips up to her shoulders bared but for the narrow straps. "Okay, if I keep moving?"

"Yes, of course." Stop him? Never!

"Good." His glide moved along the tops of her shoulders and to the base of her neck, where he toyed with her hair and earlobes. "I know couples connect, but do they really…simply…touch?

We have sex with our lovers and that's…sex. How often do we slow down and linger on the curve of our partner's earlobe?"

Maeve wanted to sigh but she held it back. The caress of her earlobe was weirdly erotic and— she had never had a man do such a thing to her. Sex truly was a strange act that two people seemed to fall into and perform as if by rote.

Hello, I'm horny, let's satisfy one another but not really look into one another's eyes.

"Taking the time to explore should be first and foremost," she whispered.

"Exactly." He nuzzled his nose into her hair, burnishing along her neck. "You smell good. Like spring and vanilla."

"You smell like royal violet and the earth."

He smiled against her neck, and his fingers pulled back her hair to fully expose her neck. "Right. My color. I would expect nothing less from one so ridiculously obsessed with color. But your dress…"

"My dress?"

"You said earlier it was a cautionary color."

"My mood has changed since I put it on. Now the color has blossomed into a lush, juicy…" Now she did meet his gaze in the mirror. The room light was as low as candlelight, but his smile over the top of her shoulder warmed her to her bones. "Desire. Keep touching me?"

"I couldn't stop now if I wanted to."

Allowing herself to relax, to take in every molecule of the man's presence, Maeve dropped her shoulders as his hands moved down her spine and to her waist. While he did so, his head remained near hers, and…the kiss to her neck was utterly soul spinning. Asher's mouth opened against the tender rise along her vein and his tongue crept out to tickle, taste. Linger. Gasping, she bowed her head, curling into the sweet sensation that coiled in her core.

Every part of her body focused on that one spot on her neck. Her fingers curled and her thighs squeezed together. Her belly softened as she felt a tingle swirl lower. Deep violet kisses punctuated her neck. Each one shoving in that arrow lodged in her heart deeper and deeper.

One of his hands slid around her waist. A certain claiming. Maeve threaded her fingers through his. She wanted to turn around and touch him, to run her fingers through his hair, to…relax even more into the sure climax that teased at her. But it was too soon. Too presumptuous. And—what about the rule?

"My turn?" she said on a gasp.

"Of course."

Damn the no-sex rule.

She turned and, the intense connection breaking, took a moment to meet his gaze. There was nothing whatsoever The Face about Asher Dane at this moment. No false charm. He wasn't faking anything. The compassion and desire in his glacier-blue eyes enticed like geothermal pools. Warm and inviting. A heavenly retreat.

Maeve slid her hands up his shirt front and… unbuttoned a few more buttons. Smoothing her palms over his skin, she marveled at the hard muscle beneath and the warmth that burnished skin against skin. Asher sucked in a breath. The sound of his pleasure lured her closer, and while marveling over his hard pecs, she leaned up and kissed him.

Violet kisses warmed her soul. And ignited her craving to a heady blaze. This kiss quickly grew urgent. Not at all polite. She wouldn't want it any other way. The man's soft groan as she deepened the kiss worked like a call to her inner sex goddess. Satisfaction was required to appease that deity.

She pulled off his shirt and tossed it to the floor. He slipped down one of her dress straps. The only way more clothing was going to be removed was to take off the whole dress.

"We may be exceeding the boundaries of the assignment," she noted while she drew her fingernails lightly down his torso. The man's muscles contracted and he hissed softly. Her goddess arched her back and smiled wickedly.

"Screw the assignment." He lifted her and set her on the bed, leaning over her as he did so that she fell back against the bed. "I want you, Maeve. And this is not fake. This is real. We are…"

"Real," she finished. "Yes, I want you too. But we'll fail the assignment."

"Figured you for a studious sort."

"I've failed here and there."

"Want to fail again? With me?"

She pulled him down onto her, and he rolled her so she was on top of him. "It'll be my best failure ever."

CHAPTER FIFTEEN

A GLINT OF pale sunlight twinkled Maeve awake. It was too early by mere mortal standards. Before six. Her body protested rising so she rolled over to find Asher smiling at her.

"Morning," he said in a sleepy tone.

"Not yet. Roosters don't even rise this early. I want to cling to sleep a little longer."

"Would a kiss be too invigorating?"

She snuggled against his body, hugging her breasts to his chest and—quickly learned a part of him was very awake. She kissed his jaw and nuzzled against his neck. "It would be." But only because she didn't want her morning breath to scare him off. "Although…" She glided her hand downward. "A slow, deep hug wouldn't wake me too much."

He moved closer and they joined slowly, sweetly. "Feels right here."

"It does."

"Never fake, Maeve. I promise."

And as they moved rhythmically, she closed her eyes to the bliss of being wrapped in Asher's arms.

Asher wandered the room in his boxer briefs and out to the patio. He didn't worry that other guests would see him; each patio was screened on one side. And if someone did? Let 'em look!

Maeve, who had risen to shower after they'd made love, had then left to collect pastries for breakfast while he'd showered.

The sun had burst on the horizon. The light permeated his skin and seemed to dance with his molecules. The day felt more promising than a recently discovered lost Picasso that could net millions at auction. He had made love to Maeve, and it had felt more right than anything. Not like a fling or a hookup in a city in which he was spending a few nights to attend an auction. What he had with Maeve was mature and real, and it baffled him because—*was* this the real thing? Could he have what he desired from her? His crazy goal about family and children and happiness with a lifelong partner. He'd not initially thought of her as someone who could be a part of his life. And now he couldn't imagine making another step without her by his side.

Every clue he got from her echoed the same feeling. That she was in this for whatever came next. Would it be fair to her to attempt a relationship while he remained her boss? How would visits to the office be received by Krew and Joss if he kissed the receptionist upon arrival?

Asher shook his head. The guys wouldn't care. And he didn't care if they did care.

We know.

But the long-distance part would be difficult. Challenging. He liked what he had started with Maeve. He didn't want to rush into scenarios that made it wrong.

But there was still the reason he'd come here in the first place. Krew and Joss would not be pleased if he returned to the office kissing his receptionist sans a new artist.

He had to get on his A game today and track down Tony Kichu. But they had a day in town planned. The rehab classes were completed. A day of sightseeing offered a getaway to use their newly learned partnership skills in real life. Couples would report back later this evening and fill out questionnaires and rate the course. Then tomorrow morning was graduation, and following, the flight back to London.

As soon as he arrived at Heathrow Airport, Asher had to catch a flight to Bangladesh to attend an auction. That left him about a day to find Kichu and sign him on. He should not go into town today, but instead stay behind and stalk the guru… Though not spending the day with Maeve sounded like an even worse plan.

Might it be easier to locate Kichu while everyone was away? The man would let down his guard; maybe he'd wander about the grounds.

Asher turned to face the room. Inside, the rumpled bedsheets gave him a smile. There was yet a lot of ground to cover at the resort. If he stayed behind, he still might not find Kichu, and then he'd have lost a day spent with Maeve for nothing.

"I'll track him down this evening. It will happen."

That was his story and he was sticking to it.

Maeve waited for the elevator, a box of pastries in hand. She loved the *pain au chocolat* that was made fresh every morning. It was always warm and flaky, and the right amount of dark chocolate oozed into every bite. Asher seemed to enjoy anything she brought him, so this morning it was a choice of croissant or cream-filled donut.

Bouncing on her heels, she realized her smile had not softened since she'd risen. After a shower, she'd spun into the room to model her yellow sundress splattered with pink polka dots for Asher. Yellow for creativity and the sky was the limit. She'd bounced into a kiss with him and had promised to return as quickly as possible.

Leaving him standing there in nothing but a sheet wrapped about his hips had been difficult. They'd broken the rules last night.

Did that mean this was a real relationship? She wanted to rush ahead into that status but didn't want to make a fool of herself. It could have been a natural reaction to the touch exercise. It may not have meant as much to Asher as it did to her. In her experience, men were more physical than women. They could have sex without emotion. But herself? Sex meant something to her.

And so did Asher.

They needed to get straight about what that tousle in the sheets—twice, including this morning—had meant. Was it being too controlling on her part to want to know? She didn't want to ruin what she had with him by asking questions and making it weird.

I can make it weirder.

He seemed to understand her. So she decided to ride the moment and try not to overthink it too much. It had been sex. She needed to…go with it. Not expect a marriage proposal or life-long commitment over one night together.

When the elevator door opened, she felt the presence of another person rush to enter behind her as she got in. Turning, she aimed to press the floor button but someone she recognized beat her to it.

"First floor?" Tony Kichu asked.

"Yes, uh…Mr. Kichu. It's so nice to finally meet you. My…partner and I have really enjoyed the retreat."

"That's a lovely shade of yellow," he commented on her dress. "Creative."

Enamored that he intuited the golden color's exact meaning, she effused, "I was feeling a creative surge this morning. It also invites opportunity."

He looked at her anew. "You navigate by color?"

"Color is a big part of my life. I tend to dress emotionally."

The door opened, and he pressed the hold button, seeming interested. "I tend to wear white because it is neutral and allows me to embrace whatever the world wishes me to notice."

"And this morning you noticed me," she said, and didn't even show the inward wince at such a presumptive statement.

"Indeed. You are here with Mr. Dane? The art broker?"

"Yes, he's my…" Lover! "Partner. Well, you know that. It's why we're here, isn't it?"

Stop being so idiotic, Maeve. Use this opportunity!

"Asher mentioned he spoke to you briefly the other day. He's very interested in seeing your art."

"I don't show it to anyone."

"I'd like to see it. I mean... I love art. All art. And I'm not a dealer or someone looking to buy art. You shouldn't feel uncomfortable showing it to me."

"My work is very...particular. But it does incorporate a lot of color."

Sensing an opening, she stepped up to block the doors and matched his stance. "I do like color."

He took a while to look her over, his soft gaze taking in her hair and face and clothing. Nothing sexual, more like seeing a like soul.

"Perhaps," he said. "But you are on your way to breakfast? Or in the middle of it?" He looked to the box she held.

"It'll keep. If you have a moment right now, I'd love to see your work."

With a nod, he started to walk. "Come with me."

Having forgotten about their plans to spend the day in town, Maeve sped down the hallway toward their room. She was too excited, filled with a visceral joy at having seen Kichu's work. She'd been in his studio a mere ten minutes, but in that time she had fallen in love with his paintings. And she was the only person who had seen them? It was too amazing to comprehend!

She couldn't wait to tell Asher all about it. He was going to—

Maeve stopped abruptly in the center of the hallway, box of pastries in hand. She'd begun to think Asher would love Tony Kichu's art. But she knew better. She knew Asher's taste. He wasn't going to love the wild, busy, colorful style. It would likely be the ugliest thing he'd ever viewed.

And Asher Dane did not do ugly.

While looking over the canvases, she had briefly considered trying to win Kichu herself and bringing him to The Art Guys to show her worth. His artwork had captivated her. She would love to represent him.

Could she?

No, Maeve, you agreed to this fake relationship to help Asher nab the artist. You can't do that to him.

Only someone like…her mother would be so cruel.

It could be her means to getting what she desired.

Maeve tugged in her lower lip. What to do?

CHAPTER SIXTEEN

ASHER TEXTED THE waiting driver to give him another five minutes. Where had Maeve gotten to? She could have picked up pastries, distributed them to the entire resort and eaten her own—and his—in the time she'd been gone. He'd showered, dressed and readied for their venture into Reykjavík this morning. One final group event was scheduled for dinnertime, but otherwise all couples were heading out for a day away from classes, pottery hugging and kiss whistles.

When the door to the room opened, his anxiety fled. Maeve's bright smile summoned his return smile. But...

"We should head out," he said. "Where have you been?"

She held a box. Asher handed her the bag she'd packed earlier and reopened the door. "I was talking to someone..."

"Tell me about it in the car? The driver is waiting."

"Right, sorry. Yes, I'm excited to do some exploring. Let's go!"

Once in the back of the car, Asher gave the driver instructions to take them to the Blue Lagoon just outside Reykjavík. They planned to start the day there and then move into town for some sightseeing. He wanted it to be a romantic excursion. A way to show Maeve he really was into developing this relationship.

As the landscape sped by and they passed areas that had been recently covered by fresh lava flow from a surprisingly active volcano, he raked his fingers through his hair and then had to laugh as he finally looked at Maeve. She sat there in her cheery yellow dress, her lips pursed and her attention fixed on the scenery that swished by, holding the pastry box carefully.

She tilted a dark cherry smirk at him. "What?"

"Are you going to share those or do you want to hold them on your lap the entire day? What's got you distracted?"

"Uh, well…" She offered the box, and he took a flaky croissant. "It's nothing. For now."

"For now? Sounds ominous."

"Let's enjoy our breakfast and the day. We've been doing heavy-duty couple bonding and soul revealing all week. I want today to be light. Promising."

"Same. You said you were talking to some-one? That's why you were late?"

"Yes, just…another woman in the retreat. She's found the event very helpful. Brought her much closer to her husband."

"I've noticed a general sigh amongst the partic-ipants. Hands are being held. Voices are calmer and more respectful. Do you think…?"

Maeve gave him a *go on* look as she chewed.

"Well." He set his half-eaten croissant on the box cover she'd set between them. "We've grown closer."

She nodded, still chewing.

"Confession? I hadn't expected to get so close to you. What started as a…" He glanced to the driver, who wore dark sunglasses and could hear everything even though the radio played some weird flute music at a low volume. "You know," he said.

"A fake?"

"Yes. But, Maeve, it's not anymore. Is it?"

"Something has certainly…begun?"

"You don't sound very sure."

"I don't want to step over any lines."

"Please step, crush, shuffle, obliterate any lines you feel still exist. Maeve…" He took her hand and bowed his head to kiss it. "We've become…"

How to say it? To blurt out that he was her

boyfriend and she his girlfriend was making a large assumption. That they were a couple? Were they? He felt as though they were. But that implied so much. And it had occurred in only four days? Yes, it had happened quickly, but it felt so real, so true.

"I know what you can't say. I'm not sure I dare say it either. It could work," he said softly. "Do you want it to work?"

She nodded. "With all my heart."

"But something is still holding you back?"

"I…"

The car slowed to park as the driver cheerily announced they had arrived at the Blue Lagoon. Outside, a family toting beach bags wandered by. Asher surveyed the full parking lot, realizing this would probably not be the romantic getaway he had intended.

"It's always busy in the mornings," the driver said. "You want me to stick around for an hour or two?"

"Yes, please, if that's all right with you," Asher said.

"It's your money." The driver tapped the clock on his dashboard.

"Not a problem. Shall we?"

Maeve nodded, and with what seemed almost a regretful smile, she pushed open the door, leaving the plate with their half-eaten pastries on the seat. She bent to peer in at him.

"I do," she said. "I really do."

She closed the door and went to the trunk, which the driver popped open, to grab the bag she'd packed for them.

Asher gripped the door handle. "She does? What does she…?"

Ah. He'd asked if this relationship was something she wanted to do.

"Nice."

After a shower, Maeve met Asher in the crowded lagoon, the hot spot to visit in Iceland. The creamy blue springs steamed from the volcanic magma in the earth. It was a massive lagoon that sported stairs leading into the springs in many spots and cooling pools, saunas, a steam cave, massage waterfall, a bar that served juice, alcohol and smoothies, and even a mud mask bar where you could smear the silica-and-algae-rich mud over face and body. Hundreds of people dotted the waters.

She and Asher waded into the lukewarm water, wandering hand in hand, and eventually found a nook where one other woman floated serenely.

"This was a bad idea," Asher said.

It was. Now she was here, she could only

think about what she needed to tell him about meeting Tony Kichu.

"I should have rented us a private suite. There are too many people to relax. Not very romantic either."

She swung a look toward him. "Is it supposed to be romantic?"

"I wanted it to be." The emotion in that statement grabbed her by the heart. The Face had left the building. Only Asher remained, and man, did she adore him.

No way could she ever steal an artist from him.

She winked at him. "It is what we make it."

His smile returned. "Very well, Miss Colorful. Tell me about the color of this water. How does it affect you emotionally?"

"It's serene and yet full of mysterious energy," she said of the pale, creamy blue water. "The color makes me feel like relaxing yet at the same time as if I could run a marathon."

"Interesting." He pulled her closer to him.

Snuggling to sit on his lap, she tilted back her head and he met her with a lingering kiss. Were there people around them? She didn't notice. In Asher's arms, the rest of the world disappeared.

"What's the most interesting place you've visited on your trips to buy and sell art?" she asked.

"I love Romania. Visited Dracula's castle."

"Really? Did you suffer a bout of anemia while there?"

"No bites. But the landscape is gorgeous. And deadly. The Carpathian Mountains are jagged and dangerous, set against thick forests that a man could surely get lost in and never be discovered, except maybe by a pack of wolves. If vampires did exist, you'd find them there."

"Joss has some work there next month. A lost manuscript or something intriguing."

"Sounds right up his Indiana Jones alley. I like adventure, but when it comes to art, I prefer it dry, clean and under the best lighting. Do you think I should expand my interests? I do have a narrow field of interest when it comes to the Romantics and lush masters."

Yes, please, Maeve thought. Could he expand his interests within the next few hours so when he finally saw Tony Kichu's art he wouldn't freak out? Because one of them certainly had to sign him on with The Art Guys. She had to tell him about her meeting with him. Yet Kichu hadn't wanted to see Asher until tomorrow.

"I need to prove myself to the guys, Maeve. I've put this evening aside to locate Kichu and work my charm on him. And frankly, I've been questioning the whole power of The Face lately."

"You do know it's not your good looks that get you by, don't you?" She understood that he did indeed think that. Ingrained in him after being released from a compassionate caring mission for his parents. He'd not taken anything for himself. And now The Face wanted whatever he could grasp. "Asher, you have so much care and concern for others that it permeates everything you do."

"I don't know about that."

"You sacrificed years of your life caring for your parents. And it's not something that you utilized just for them. I see it in you all the time. Sure, you're a handsome guy. But it's what's in here—" she pressed her palm over his heart "—that other people feel when they are around you. They sense your compassion. Your intense love for the art, which is a language you speak so well. The Face is not Asher Dane. And Asher Dane is the guy who ultimately wins the auctions and appeals to his followers."

He smirked and shook his head. "You have a ridiculous obsession with me, Marsha."

"Maybe I do."

An obsession that she'd gotten to indulge in this week. An obsession that prodded her to cheer him on and do what she could to ensure he got what he came here for. This trip had been for Asher, and she wanted to see him succeed.

"I have something to tell you. I thought it could wait, but it's too remarkable not to spill. I wasn't talking to someone from the retreat when I was late."

"Oh?"

"It's amazing news, and I would have told you right away, but you were in a hurry to leave and I didn't want to tell you with the driver listening… And it's not going to happen until tomorrow anyway…"

"What *were* you doing while on the hunt for pastries?"

"I met Tony Kichu in the elevator."

"Maeve," he breathed. His eyes brightened.

"I told him I was there with you and that I loved art and—he took me to see his artwork."

Asher gripped her by the upper arms. "He did?" A variety of emotions played over his face, from surprise to excitement to concern. He swiped a hand over his hair, which was beaded with moisture from the steaming water. "What went down? What did it look like? Tell me everything!"

"He wants to meet with you tomorrow morning after the closing ceremony."

"He does?"

She nodded. "I said you could be the only one to represent him." She had to believe that for herself as well. This was Asher's win, not hers. "What with your eye for detail and color, he could trust you."

"That's so generous of you."

"It's the truth. I mean, his art is amazing. He showed me five canvases. They are so colorful! And—they are modern art, for sure. Lots of spatters and geometrics, but also, some incredible freestyle networks that run through the backgrounds. It's hard to describe. Oh, Asher, I felt so much looking at them. They spoke to me. You have to represent Kichu."

"I will. I mean, I'll have to assess the art, but judging by your enthusiasm I'm sure I'll like the work."

"Well." With a wince, she spread her arms across the surface of the water to put a little distance between them. "There is a problem."

"What's that?"

"It's not your thing. Not…beautiful."

He screwed on a disbelieving face. "Come on, Maeve, my taste doesn't always tend toward beauty."

She recounted some of the masters he loved. "Waterhouse, Millais, Rossetti, Woolner. And that's just the Pre-Raphaelite Brotherhood. Don't get me started on the entire sixteenth century. You love those artists."

"Because they are beautiful—oh." He looked aside. Realizing what he'd said? Trying to conjure one artist who wasn't considered aesthetically beautiful? "Well, there's…"

While he considered which artists he favored who were not renowned for their beauty and lushness, Maeve sank up to her chin in the blue water. She could tell that his meeting with Kichu was not going to go well.

"Don't you think I've got an open enough mind to embrace all styles?" he asked. Maeve felt the accusation in his tone. A touch of challenge, even. "Do you agree with Hammerstill? That I'm all surface and no substance?"

His defenses had gone up. And she was to blame.

"Oh, Asher, not at all. I shouldn't have made it sound as if you wouldn't be interested. You are going to love Kichu's work as much as I do, I'm sure. You've got this." She took his hand and squeezed it. "I know you do."

He nodded. Let out a reluctant exhale. Not entirely a believer in what she'd said?

Once again, she was handling his life in the background. And she wasn't sure if she'd made it better or worse with that interference.

In town they stopped in a quaint shopping area, and Maeve dragged Asher through a few Nordic clothing shops. She purchased a paisley scarf dyed a bright turquoise, violet and yellow. And when she spied a pair of expensive bright pink heels, he bought them for her. She'd initially said no. It had taken but a kiss for her to concede. He liked earning her smile as he'd handed her the bag. Something so simple as a pair of shoes brightened her entire face. He wouldn't mind having her face in his life all the time. Truly. She was the most beautiful piece of artwork in his life.

Leading him out of the shop, she pulled him down the sidewalk. They passed a gallery with a closed sign on it. No paintings inside, only a sculpture or two.

His tastes went beyond the beautiful. Didn't they? Did she think he might not have a chance at winning Kichu as a client? He couldn't help feeling offended by that. Was this how it felt to let someone in? It annoyed him. But also, it was a strange sort of ache that niggled at his armor and punctured a hole in it, allowing that kindness she saw in him to leak out. Maeve was teaching him to recognize that earthy ugliness his professor had once insisted he get in touch with.

And honestly? He liked it.

Inside a souvenir shop, Maeve floated toward the back, drawn by kitschy colorful items. Asher spun a rack of postcards, browsing photos of the town, handmade dolls, tables set with traditional food. When finally one with a colorful rock outside a parked RV popped up. The rock wasn't painted, but rather it looked as though someone had crocheted a riot of colored yarn about it. The caravan was plastered with various logos for rock bands. Before it stood a lanky man in overalls holding a wooden staff.

"Ugly," Asher muttered. With a smile, he selected the postcard.

Then, he gave the rack another spin and a card with a swirl of pastel colors that looked like AI art stood out. He plucked it out and went to pay for them.

Maeve met him at the doorway.

"You got postcards?" she asked, seeming surprised that he would.

"One for you." He tucked the ugly postcard inside his suit coat pocket then gave the other to her. "It screams Maeve Pemberton, don't you think?"

She studied the wild colors and laughed. "There may be hope for you, after all, Mr. Dane."

Back at the resort, the evening meal was delivered to their rooms. They dined on the patio, watching the sun set in vivid violet, pink and orange above the mossy volcanic field.

"I'm going to remember this sky," Maeve said, sipping the dregs of her wine. "I might have to paint a wall those colors."

"Heaven forbid." Asher, noticing her gape, quickly added, "I mean...what wall?"

Maeve laughed. If the man ever saw her flat, he might have a heart attack. An art attack? It would disturb him, for sure.

She shrugged. "With Lucy moving out, I feel the urge to try something new in the bathroom. The sunrise colors are similar to the ones on this postcard." She'd set the postcard he'd given her on the table. "You never showed me yours."

He tugged out the card and handed it to her with a churlish smile on his face. It was...

"Seriously?" she asked.

"Pretty ugly, eh?"

"I'm impressed. Asher Dane does have an eye for ugly art. Though, I wouldn't call this art."

"Certainly not. But it makes me think. Maybe I've spent too much time coasting through art and not allowing myself to really breathe it."

"You breathe art, Asher. I've watched you."

"Yes, but only the stuff I deign to be worthy. Time to expand my horizons?"

"Oh, I hope so." She tilted her glass toward him, and they met in a *ting*.

"I'm excited for tomorrow's meeting with Kichu. You did this for me, Maeve. You were the one who got his attention and convinced him to show me his art. I've failed you as a teacher. But you have achieved the task on your own. Bravo!"

"You are not a failure, and I will take that bravo. I'm excited as well. I really love his work. It speaks to me in the color language I know. So. Who's sleeping on the floor tonight?"

"Are you teasing me?"

"Yes. I'll take the floor."

His jaw dropped open.

Maeve's laughter increased to shrieks of joy as he lunged for her, grabbed her by the waist and hefted her over his shoulder to carry her inside. "We'll see about that," he announced, and then tossed her on the bed.

CHAPTER SEVENTEEN

THE FINAL CEREMONY was silly to Asher. The couples were called to the front of the room, embraced one another and received red roses from the lead instructor. Kichu watched from a video screen. Was it really that difficult for the man to make an appearance for his own event? Since when could a recluse even make a living, let alone a fortune, as a renowned relationship coach?

Well, he supposed this week had improved his relationship with Maeve. Hell, it had *given* him a relationship with Maeve. Sex again this morning had been so right. Like he didn't have to perform to impress a woman, nor did he need to cater to her unknown needs. Maeve was very vocal, and she'd even directed his hand here and there. He loved that. The communication between them was instinctual. At least between the sheets.

As for when they were fully clothed and preparing to leave the resort in a few hours? Both of them were quiet as they prepped for the meeting with Kichu. Maeve was packing and making the bed, despite him reminding her that was a job for the maid. She tended to neaten everything behind the scenes. Even his life.

Maeve had been responsible for this meeting with Kichu. He owed her. And yet, the only thing she needed, she wouldn't take from him. What was money? A loan that she could use to start her business? To him, it would barely make a dent on his ledger. And really, if she would accept a loan, there was no way he would ask for repayment.

Did she feel as though he were trying to buy his way into her life? Maeve was independent. And he knew if she had the opportunity to reopen the shop she'd dreamed about she would be a success. And her mother would be…

Well, that was the kicker. Maeve wanted to please a domineering mother. Asher couldn't relate to that. But then again, he had dropped everything in his life to care for his parents. He believed children should honor, respect and care for their parents. And Maeve was obviously trying to honor hers by showing her she could be a success.

"She won't fail," he said to his reflection in the bathroom mirror. He swiped the razor along his jaw to remove some missed stubble.

Now, as he adjusted his tie and hair, Maeve fluttered in to touch up her lipstick, her hair, her dress. The big event was happening in less than an hour. And she looked…

"Stunning." He turned and caught her hand before she could flit back into the other room. "Maeve, you are beautiful." But the announcement made him frown. He released her hand. "That color…"

"Green is my happy color," she said and floated out into the main room, leaving him to turn and face the mirror again.

Beauty was his thing? She'd been adamant about that. Listing all his favorite artists, who, indeed, had produced some of the most beautiful works over the centuries.

Of course, beauty was his thing. It had served him well through the years. There was nothing wrong with admiring a beautiful artwork. But that wasn't all he admired. Though, to think on it, there were no masters he could name that produced anything but beauty.

And he did know ugly when he saw it. Matsys, Goya, Chagall, just to consider a few of the masters. And don't even get him started on the modern artists. Leave those works to others who could understand the horrible dysfunction immortalized on the canvas.

He glanced to the postcard he'd propped against the mirror. What of all the things that were not beautiful? That were weird and strange and intriguing?

You must become open to the earthy and ugly.

Maeve was not ugly. Maeve was a unique beauty. She was…earthy and colorful and studious and simple and complicated. He'd never quite been able to look at her and figure her out for her eclectic color scheme, but she had grown on him this week. Because he now understood what made her tick. And she wouldn't be Maeve Pemberton if she were not a wild riot of mismatched colors and patterns. He wouldn't have her any other way.

Could his taste in art alter in such a manner? Be opened to looking beyond the surface beauty? To accept that which he deemed ugly?

His ego loomed behind it all. An ego that had escaped its chains after years of tending his sick parents. A part of him that had wanted to be seen and recognized had taken control. Had successfully brought the media and masses to The Art Guys and made them a name. Yes, he'd take credit for that.

Honestly? He didn't need that credit any longer. He could do with less. No fame. Maybe a little. The fame and notice he received did transfer to the brokerage. What Maeve said about it not always being about him was true. Through the years he'd sucked it all up, shining in the attention. Was that why he'd never taken on an artist? Because to do so meant allowing that artist to shine, to step aside and allow the spotlight a new muse.

Wow. He suddenly got it.

The Face must be set aside. He simply wanted to be Asher Dane, a man who loved art—and was open to seeing all kinds in a new light—and who adored a woman with multitudes of color in her eyes and punctuation marks at her mouth.

"I've developed a ridiculous obsession with Maeve," he whispered.

"What's that? Are you ready?" She popped her head back into the bathroom. "That tie is perfect. The violet is your color."

"It is?" He touched the tie but was lost in her strange beauty. Maeve was the key to escape his self-imposed artificial world of beauty and expectations.

"It is. It's the color I see when I smell your delicious youness."

"My youness? You mean my cologne? It's… specially made for me."

"Of course, it wouldn't be anything you could buy off the shelf. I love it."

She kissed him, and all he could think was that he wished she'd said she loved him.

Ending the kiss with a quick one to his nose, she grabbed his hand. "Let's go snag you a new artist."

As they strolled hand in hand toward the elevator, Maeve checked her texts. She'd received a confirmation from the job application, and it indicated the date for their online interview. Next Monday! That was three days from now. And... she wasn't prepared.

Had she really thought it a good idea to look for another job?

What was a good reason to not confirm? She'd changed her mind? She didn't want to move away from a man she had begun to have a relationship with? Dublin held no interest for her? She had decided to tough it out for a few more years to see if she could rise in the ranks at The Art Guys?

"Your mum?" Asher asked as the elevator doors slid open.

"No, just..."

She couldn't tell him she'd applied for a job. It had been a spur of the moment decision to create some means of backup, a place to fall should she find herself back at the reception desk without a raise or a future that indicated she could accomplish her dream.

"It's to the right," she directed as Asher stepped out of the elevator.

Tucking away her phone, she thought about how he kept his turned off most of the time. She should have left hers in the room today. Now she would be even more nervous about this meeting. Because a yay or a nay from Kichu might decide her future.

CHAPTER EIGHTEEN

ASHER SHOOK HANDS with the elusive Tony Kichu and took in his simple white kimono, loose slacks and long obsidian hair, a portion of which was pulled into a topknot at the back of his skull. Behind him were displayed a Japanese gold Satsuma vase and other collectibles situated prominently in his main living area. Maeve, after shaking his hand, wandered to inspect the tall vase, leaning forward but keeping her hands behind her back.

Green was her happy color? And violet for him? Those colors were complimentary.

When he realized Kichu had spoken but he'd not caught what he said, Asher had to yank himself from his thoughts about Maeve—*his ridiculous obsession*—and focus.

"So, shall we take a look at your work?" Asher asked.

"Of course. This way." Kichu strolled on bare feet down a long white hallway that featured what Asher guessed were Ming vases set into

MICHELE RENAE   217

the walls and lighted perfectly. He wasn't an expert on ancient pottery. "The two of you work together?"

"Yes," Maeve said. "As I told you, Asher is my boss."

"We've been dating four or five months," Asher added with a look to her for reassurance. Best to keep up the cover. He didn't want to reveal their fake relationship when he was so close to finally seeing the art.

"About that," Maeve agreed.

"An excellent program you have here," Asher said to Kichu's back. "I'll be recommending it to my friends."

Kichu paused before an open doorway and gestured inside. "My studio."

Asher waited for Maeve to enter first, then took in the vast room. One side was all windows looking out over the steaming geothermal pools and the periwinkle sky. Canvases lined one wall, some propped on the floor, others set on wooden easels. A blank canvas sat at the center of the room, stretches of paint-spattered clothes covering the marble floor. But the most shocking sight was the vast array of paint. Everywhere. In every color. Splattered and splotched and smeared and stroked.

Asher blinked. It was as if he had to mentally guide himself to breathe a lower amount of oxygen. There was so much color it sucked away his breath. At first glance he didn't realize the splotches and splatters were canvases. Finished works?

Veins tightening, his fingers clenched. The sanctity of art itself had been trampled, graffitied and blown up. Splattered like a runny egg thrust at the wall. Crushed from a tube of oil paint and drizzled indiscriminately. Blocks of color showed thick brush strokes, blending olive and yellow and crimson and—

This was not art! This was…a mess. A child's tantrum. A—

Swallowing back the oath that climbed up his throat, Asher noticed Maeve's hopeful smile and the bounce on her toes as she awaited his summation. She in her happy summer green and cherry lips. Of course she would find this chaos beautiful. It emulated her mind!

Forcing a smile, Asher approached the paintings. If one could call them that. There were similarities to Pollock's splatter paintings, but not so ordered or even intentional. Influences of Shimamoto were also evident. Yet what the man had done with color was an aberration. How could Maeve actually…? No, he didn't have to wonder. This must be her Xanadu.

Kichu joined him to stand side by side. The

man's quiet presence felt too soft and gentle for this crazy explosion and utter waste of paint.

"I know my style is not for everyone," Kichu said. "It is why I rarely show my work."

"But so many would love to own your work," Maeve stated from the other side of Asher. "The use of color is…arrogant."

Asher flashed her a stunned look. She'd got that one right.

"Yet," she continued, "inviting. It speaks in whispers and screams. And takes the viewer to such intense places. Don't you think, Asher?"

No, he did not think!

But, hell. He sensed she was offering him a means to ingratiate himself to Kichu. She had warned him he wouldn't like the works. And he did not. She knew him so well. That fortified his heart and very soul. And he didn't want to lose her regard.

And yet, he could feel Maeve's insistent hope in the tone of her voice. She needed him to like Kichu's art for reasons… Well, she might return to London having helped him to gain an artist. That would show well to the other guys. They may agree it was time to allow her to move beyond the reception desk.

On the other hand, if her taste was so terrible, Asher wasn't sure he could agree on that promotion at the brokerage.

And really, did she harbor notions that he hadn't the constitution to represent such an utter blemish on modern art itself?

He swore inwardly. This retreat had opened his heart and shifted his perspective. He needn't rely on beauty and surface looks to succeed. To get others to like him. To exist. As well, he'd fallen for Maeve. His strange yet beautiful Maeve. He didn't want to let her down.

And yet...

He had also learned to be truthful on this retreat, for perhaps the first time in his life. And he if lied now he may regret it forever.

"It's ugly," he announced.

Maeve's inhale alerted him. But he couldn't represent art he could not connect to.

"Thank you for your honesty," Kichu said. "You are the first person who has had the courage to tell me the truth. I appreciate that."

"It's not without artistic value," Asher found himself saying. "But it's...not something I can represent. I'm sorry." He shook Kichu's hand. "I won't take up any more of your time. Thank you for this week. It's taught me a lot."

Kichu nodded silently.

"But maybe if you thought about it a few days," Maeve said even as Asher turned to exit. "It is a wild riot of unexpected color, but you've learned to appreciate..."

He paused at the door, knowing the word she did not say was *me*. Yes, he'd learned to appreciate her. He'd gone beyond appreciation. And now, as her mouth dropped and she blinked, he couldn't find the path to that easy acceptance she'd offered him.

She shook Kichu's hand. "I'm so sorry. I do love your work. I'd love to… Well, you'll find someone who can represent it, I'm sure of it."

I'd love to…

She'd love to represent Kichu's work? Asher felt surely if anyone could manage to look at the work any longer than a glance it would be Maeve. Yet, she had no experience whatsoever in representing an artist. And he certainly wasn't the man to teach her. Because what experience had he? He was still zero for zero when it came to acquiring artists. And perhaps even she had led him here knowing the outcome? What was she playing at?

Pity they'd wasted all this time for this disastrous result.

Asher held out his hand for Maeve and called another thanks to Kichu as she approached him. She didn't take his hand. Instead, she rushed past him. He had to step rapidly to keep up with her. When they landed in the hallway outside Kichu's private apartment, she started to run.

"Maeve! Let's talk about this!"

"Our car arrives in half an hour."

Yes, they had a flight this afternoon. Back to London for Maeve. But for him it was only a layover as he headed to Bangladesh.

She was upset he'd not liked Kichu's work. And...he didn't know how to make this situation better.

CHAPTER NINETEEN

ON THE DRIVE to the airport, Maeve scrolled through her emails. A means to look busy and not talk. She told Asher that Joss had an issue with a reservation—which he did—and that took some time to work out.

Once seated in first class and with a glass of wine in hand, she wanted to close her eyes and try not to inhale Asher's royal violet essence. Impossible. The man had permeated her bones. She felt sure she'd smell him, feel him on her skin, at her lips, even when she was home and he had arrived in Bangladesh.

One thing to be thankful for, this exit would be swift after they arrived home, not drawn out with them sharing a cab from the airport to their respective homes. And then having to wonder if they dared to suggest one might go home with the other?

The relationship felt...not completely true. Unsustainable. Perhaps as false as it had begun.

By rejecting Kichu's artwork, Asher had rejected *her*. In that moment, when Asher had said the word *ugly*, and she'd watched Kichu bow his head and nod in reluctant acceptance, Maeve had felt that exchange as a knife in her heart. Gone were the Cupid-drawn love arrows. Asher's verbal blade had stabbed deep and sure.

Of course, she had known he wouldn't like the art. It wasn't his style. It was weird. It was too colorful. It challenged the aesthetic beauty he worshipped.

Tony Kichu's art…was *her*.

And once again she had failed.

She had failed to help Asher procure an artist. She had failed to show him that viewing the artwork in a new light could result in an appreciation for it. She had failed to prove that she was of value to the team and deserved a raise, a new position that would see her thriving and achieving her dream.

Might *she* have offered to represent Kichu? No, she wasn't in a position to do so. And Asher may have taken that as a direct assault against their work relationship. The last thing she'd wanted to do was hurt him. Or ruin his chances at proving himself to his coworkers.

As she glanced at the text on her phone, her heart dropped even lower. Of all the people to contact her when she was feeling lowest. Her mother. Asking about the Dublin job.

"Listen, Maeve, I'm sorry."

She swiped to ignore the text and tilted her head against the airplane headrest. "You don't need to apologize to me, Asher. It's been a long week. I'm tired."

"Is that your way of saying you don't want to discuss it? We need to. We…"

His heavy sigh echoed in her bones. Because he lived there, and she felt every part of him, every emotion, every movement, every sound, smell and sigh. She wanted to grip him by the shoulders and yell at him.

See me! Accept me! I am that weird colorful woman who baffles you still.

He had been so close to seeing her.

"Tell me what I've done wrong," he said in a soft but desperate tone.

Maeve winced. If he didn't know, that was half the problem.

She could play the spurned lover and sit there silently ignoring him—but that didn't play well with her soul.

"It was…" She thought it through. "I knew you wouldn't like Kichu's work. Perhaps I should have prepared you better."

"Maeve, you are not responsible for my work or the clients I represent. Sure, I failed to snag Kichu as an artist. There will be other opportunities for me to show the guys I can bring in artists."

"I loved his work. It spoke to me."

"All those colors. I know it did. And in that moment when I was looking at it, I wondered if I should lie and say I loved it. That I'd represent him. I knew that would make you happy. But... I've learned some things about myself this week. And being honest with the way I present myself to others is a big part of it. I had to tell the truth."

She appreciated his honesty, but it still hurt.

"You make me feel..." He rubbed the back of his head in frustration. "Honestly? I felt like you've had my back this whole time, and then in Kichu's workshop you were trying to force his art on me. Like you didn't trust I could form my own opinion. It felt a little...underhanded."

Maeve swallowed. She hadn't meant to convey that at all. But if he'd felt that way she had to honor that feeling. She had only tried to encourage him to view the art in...in the manner she viewed it.

"I'm sorry," she said. And she really was. "I was trying to subtly influence you."

He turned his head on the headrest to eye her, their faces but inches apart. If he didn't smell so deliciously violet this would be much easier for her. But fact was, she'd lost her heart to him this week. And then he'd crushed it. And now he was acting as though that trampling couldn't possibly matter as much as it did.

And very likely she had done some trampling herself.

"When does your connecting flight leave from London?" she asked.

She knew that he had to hop on a plane to Bangladesh for an auction tomorrow morning.

"If we land on time, I'll have about twenty minutes to dash to the next gate."

Her phone pinged again, and she tugged it out to check the screen. She knew that was rude, but the distraction was very needed. It was a confirmation for the interview time.

"Joss again?"

"No, I ironed things out for him. It's… Asher, I sent in an application yesterday for a marketing job in Dublin. This is a confirmation for an online interview."

His gasp hurt her heart. She didn't want it to go like this. But she wasn't sure they had a future anymore. Most especially, her future at The Art Guys felt stagnant.

"I'll talk to the guys," he said. "We'll give you a raise."

"I don't want it handed to me because you think that's a way to…" Please her? Keep her at the brokerage? If only he did want to keep her! "I'm not sure we can work. We're so different."

"Maeve, differences make for a vibrant relationship. Is it me?"

She inhaled and bowed her head. Of course, it was him! She desired everything about him. Was she being too harsh? Too judgmental? Perhaps he might come around? Really. It had been one artist. An artist she'd known he wouldn't like. Why her need to stick to this one point?

Because it felt like rejection.

"I need to sort this all out," she said. "Maybe you leaving so quickly is a good thing. To give me space to get my head straight."

"Straight about us? Because, Maeve, I…"

He couldn't say it. Because he wasn't so sure about their relationship anymore.

Asher Dane didn't understand her, after all. He could never handle the colorful and weird Maeve Pemberton.

"You are strange and beautiful," he said.

She lifted her gaze to meet his. "What?"

"You are a little strange. Not in a bad way. Just in that supernatural, colorful, beaming out green and fuchsia and orange in your special way kind of strange. I get that. I understand how you navigate the world. And I want to embrace it. I've tried to…"

He pressed a hand over her heart chakra. Maeve lifted her chin to stop the tears that threatened. It was too late. Wasn't it?

Their differences might never coalesce.

* * *

The moment the plane hit the tarmac Asher's heart dropped lower than the airplane had. Maeve immediately busied herself with the luggage. Was she avoiding him? He sensed she was angry over his rejection of Kichu. Not at *him*.

He hoped that was the case.

And yet, she had a job interview? Something she'd applied for while at the retreat? Had she been plotting behind his back the whole time? Setting up a means for backup should the ploy to recruit Kichu not come to fruition? He should have asked her more about it, but he didn't know how to deal with upset Maeve.

He wondered what color represented her current mood. Certainly not the green dress she wore, and which she'd said was the color she most identified with.

As they disembarked and walked through the Jetway, he wanted to pull Maeve into his arms and tell her he loved her. But did he love her?

He felt as though he did. This weird tiff over Kichu was messing with his mind. Making him question the entire week. *Had* it all been fake, after all? If she intended to interview for another job and leave him…

His phone pinged, alerting him that his next flight was boarding.

Maeve paused with her rolling suitcase and met his gaze. "You need to run," she said.

"I can't walk away from you like this. I... I'll miss my flight. We need to talk."

"You need to be at that auction tomorrow morning. The client depends on you. I'll be fine to catch a cab on my own."

"It's not that..." His phone pinged again. Asher swore. He did need to run.

Leaning in to kiss her, he winced as Maeve turned her head so his mouth landed on her cheek. "I'll text you."

"Thanks for the week," she said softly. Then she grabbed her suitcase and walked away.

And with another ping from his phone, Asher began to walk backward, unable to tear his sight from the woman who had stolen a part of him with her apostrophe smiles. And she was taking that part with her now. He didn't want it back. But he wasn't sure how to make things right. Should he fall before Kichu and apologize and offer to represent him? That wouldn't sit well with his heart.

Nor Maeve's. She'd know he was only doing it to please her, and that was unacceptable.

Turning, he began to run toward his next gate.

Maeve hailed a cab and gave the driver an address to a location she'd been meaning to visit.

It was around nine in the evening, but she didn't want to go home yet. Lucy was on a weekend getaway with her fiancé so the flat would be dark, lonely and too quiet.

Hugging herself, she tilted her head back and zoned out on the flashes of city lights zipping by. Asher's flight was probably already in the air. They hadn't time to say a proper goodbye.

The real goodbye had been said in Tony Kichu's studio when Asher had called the artist's work ugly. Maeve had felt that in her being. Everything Kichu had created resembled a piece of her life, a colorful burst of her very soul.

So this was the end? A quick kiss in the airport and a promise to text? It felt dismissive. Not hopeful. Not as if she could claim him as anything more than a man with whom she'd had a good time and… Now back to their roles as boss and receptionist. And she couldn't abide a friends-with-benefits relationship with anyone, most of all Asher Dane. It was all or nothing.

She felt as though she had fallen hard and splattered across the ground in all the colors of Kichu's brilliant canvases.

Wiping away a tear, she inhaled and composed herself. She could come up with a new plan to a better future. To continue to work at The Art Guys. But how to do so and be around Asher? Krew and Joss had been so kind to her.

Truly, she did feel like *our Maeve*. Like they were a family apart from her broken real family.

But Asher didn't fit properly into that weird and makeshift family. She knew how she wanted him to fit. But it seemed he wasn't ready for such an adjustment.

Was the job interview more of an excuse to exit gracefully from Asher's life than a real goal? She didn't want to move back to Dublin. Her home was... Well, she wouldn't call London home. Sure, her da lived here. They got together a few times a year. New York was where her mum lived when she wasn't traveling. Again, she never saw her more than a few times a year.

You've failed again!

She had failed to help Asher get the artist. Failed to move up at work. And she had failed to get the guy who made her heart dance and glow purple and green.

"This is the place."

Alerted by the cabbie's voice, Maeve glanced outside. A streetlight shone over the vacant shop front sandwiched between a record shop and a plant emporium. It had come on the market two weeks ago. It wouldn't remain available for long. The storefront was pristine and painted a sallow mint, which she would refresh with pink and ochre stripes.

"Do you want to get out?"

"Uh, no. Can you take me to another place? I've a list that I want to check out." She gave him the next address on her running list of dream shop locations. And she didn't arrive home until after two in the morning.

Stepping into her dark flat, Maeve let her suitcase drop as she closed the door. No one to greet her and welcome her home. She wanted that. A place where she felt welcome, loved. A family.

But more than anything she wanted to feel the warm acceptance she'd felt standing in Asher's arms. A place she'd thought her colorful world fit.

CHAPTER TWENTY

AFTER ASHER WON the auction, his client had asked if he'd stay for a few days to catch another private sale, which he was happy to do. It wasn't the commission that attracted him, but rather the mutual taste in art and the pints they shared at a local pub later. As well, the client knew a local artist who was looking for representation. Asher had an appointment to meet with him in an hour.

Joss and Krew had taken the news that he'd refused to represent Tony Kichu with their standard accepting, "You'll find one sooner or later." Passing over Kichu hadn't felt so much like a failure as a letdown. Asher was not holding up his part of the partnership. He'd been so close. But to be truthful with himself, he was good with not taking on Kichu. He'd been honest in a moment when a simple lie could have gained him prestige with the brokerage and…won the girl.

Maeve would have seen through him if he'd

taken on Kichu. She knew him better than he knew himself some days. She saw Asher Dane, not The Face. He wanted to make Maeve proud. Had he lost that chance? In the three days since they'd parted, he'd been so busy he'd only managed to text her regarding some client paperwork.

Now, as he sat in his hotel room nursing a chilled whiskey, he could tap out a few words to her. But he let his phone sit in a suit coat pocket across the room. She had asked for time to think. About them? About leaving the brokerage? Hell, he shouldn't have blurted out that he'd give her more money to keep her at The Art Guys. That had been an act of desperation. Maeve was too smart to fall for that.

And he was too smart to treat her heart so poorly. He had to be true to his newly opened heart. A heart Maeve had been successful in brushing off, polishing up and hugging—around pottery—until he knew that nothing else mattered but what she thought of him. His self-esteem had gotten a new polish as well. He didn't have to be The Face around Maeve. And he felt sure Asher Dane could be present more often than The Face as he moved forward in his work.

Why hadn't he immediately realized that by rejecting Tony Kichu's art he was also rejecting Maeve? It had not hit him until they'd been sitting on the plane and she had confessed to trying to influence him. Maeve had adored the crazy splattered work that Asher couldn't even begin to understand. But that was the thing, wasn't it? He hadn't understood Maeve Pemberton either, until he'd spent time with her. Learned her.

What *did* she think of him? Could she see that he was gaining self-esteem? That he no longer felt the need to wear The Face as a mask? He'd rejected Kichu's work and had survived. No false charm necessary.

But that rejection had hurt Maeve. He'd thought of her every moment since he'd had to dash away from her. He abhorred the distance between him and the one thing that made his heart sing.

A woman of many colors. All he desired was to become her favorite color.

He must make things right between them. And he knew how to do that. Lunging for his phone, he dialed the resort and, after utilizing The Face's charm, was put through to Tony Kichu. The man defensively announced that he'd refused Hammerstill's offer of representation and wouldn't consider Asher again. Although, he did know who he would like to represent him.

It made sense. And it made Asher happy. With that initial discomfiting bit of business out of the way, he spent the next half hour convincing Kichu to create a commissioned work for him.

* * *

Maeve signed off from the video interview and headed in to work. The interview had gone well. Maybe?

Didn't matter. She didn't want the Dublin job. Yet she felt as though she needed it as backup. The interviewer had sounded interested and fascinated by her love for color. She said she'd get back in a week; there was a list of potential applicants she had to interview.

Fair enough.

The office was dark when she arrived after 10:00 a.m. Joss was away on a job and Krew had auctions in town all week. She flicked on the lights and eyed her half-circle desk. She loved that desk. It was curvy and highlighted by gentle overhead lights. The command center from which she ran the office. And she did it well.

With a sigh, she set her purse under the desk and pulled up a project on the computer. Krew had received a list of paintings to bid on at auction for a wealthy client who was recently divorced. The vindictive wife had sold all their artwork while he had been waiting to win the right to keep the home and the art. Now he wanted it back, at all costs. It would prove an art scavenger hunt. Exactly the sort of assignment the analytical yet competitive Krew would enjoy.

Looking aside from the spreadsheet she was

creating for the art hunt, Maeve caught her chin
in hand and stared out the window at the gray
sky. Rain was due within a few hours. Fitting,
because life felt colorless since landing in London days earlier.

She hadn't spoken to Asher, though she had
answered two of his texts regarding a hotel snafu
and had sent paperwork to him to have his client sign. He hadn't mentioned anything about…
them.

Why should he?

Maeve sighed. She'd lost him. And she wasn't
sure how to get him back. Could she run away
from it all and focus on her dreams instead of
the hole in her heart that seemed to widen daily?

She had fallen in love with Asher Dane. And
it wasn't fake. Or some silly crush fantasy. But
he was not a color that seemed to fit into her
world. A rich dusty violet. The color of royalty,
midnight gardens, bejeweled insects and…the
man who had pulled a gray cloud over her heart.

Four days later, Maeve was offered the job as
marketing director for the Dublin office. To start
in two weeks. Would she accept?

Leaning back in her chair, with Krew's voice
muted in the background as he spoke behind the
closed door with a client, she stared at the email
that had new-hire paperwork attached for her to

fill out and sign. The pay was nearly double what she was making right now. A few years there would allow her to save enough to open another shop. It was the path to her dream.

At the expense of walking away from something she loved. It wasn't this job that called to her heart. Though she did take pride in it, and adored Joss and Krew. They really were her family. A family she hadn't dared to tell that she was looking for other work. Had Asher mentioned it to them? Krew hadn't said anything. And she hadn't seen Joss since returning to London.

"This failing stuff is exhausting," she muttered.

But then she sat up straighter and shook her head. If she had learned anything this week it was that she viewed the world differently than others. And that her perspective should not rely on the opinions of others. Yes, her mum considered her a failure. But Asher did not. In fact, he'd convinced her that she was merely learning, gliding in her own way toward what she desired.

She had been labeling her life incorrectly! And if her mum insisted on seeing her in one way, then so be it. Maeve didn't require her seal of approval. Because Mariane Pemberton's approval was only granted through her purview of what was success and what was failure.

"I will open another shop," she said with exacting determination. "It'll happen when it needs to happen."

She wanted to thank Asher for changing her perspective. He was due in town today. He didn't need to stop by the office. She wasn't sure if she wanted him to or not.

Yes, she did want to see him. But could her heart handle looking into his glacier-blue eyes and wondering if she had thrown away the best thing she had ever had?

They should talk. Maybe this could all be ironed out with a heartfelt conversation. Or maybe the man would simply never understand her. And that was fine. She shouldn't expect him to. She didn't completely understand him. He had his ineffable parts. As did her mum. And as did Maeve Pemberton.

Clicking open the attached file on the email, she glanced through the new-hire forms, and then shook her head. She'd save it for when she got home. As long as she was in this office, her attention would be devoted to this work.

CHAPTER TWENTY-ONE

THE NEXT MORNING, Maeve adjusted the bouquet of yellow daisies she'd set on her bedroom chest of drawers. Last night after work she'd pick them up, along with a takeaway. She'd been in need of some cheer, but the daisies had not played their part. They had wilted overnight and the stems were bent. There was no saving them.

"Figures," she muttered. "Seems to be how my life is going right now."

A glance to the pink heels she'd set on the floor at the end of her bed took away her breath. Asher had insisted she have the strappy stunners. They'd go perfectly with a summery dress. And a walk with the one man who had stolen her heart.

Asher had not stopped into the office yesterday even though he'd landed at the airport midafternoon. Was he trying to avoid her? If so, she didn't want to participate in a mutual avoidance scheme for the rest of her days at The Art Guys.

Grabbing her laptop, she crawled onto her bed

and opened the new employee form. The atmosphere at the office had altered since she'd returned. Krew was apprehensive around her. Had Asher told him everything? That he'd had a fling with the receptionist and…

And what? The world felt off-kilter. And she wasn't sure where she would land should a good shake occur. In Asher's arms should be the answer. But that they'd not had opportunity to talk, nor had he reached out to her since parting at Heathrow, did not bode well.

Time to refocus on her dream. A dream that suddenly felt less colorful knowing that a dusty shade of royal violet might be absent from it.

Out in the living room, Lucy called that she'd be back later. She had a dress fitting appointment. Yet before the front door closed, Lucy also called, "You've got a visitor!"

Maeve never got visitors unless it was her da, and he usually texted that he was in the neighborhood and was stopping by.

Pulling on a pink sweater over her orange and green paisley sundress, she wandered out to the living room, unsure who could possibly be there. She stopped abruptly, catching her breath at the sight of the man standing in the doorway.

The missing color.

Behind Asher, Lucy winked at her, then closed the door as she left.

"Asher."

He set aside what looked like a large wrapped canvas. Must be something he'd acquired for work?

"Maeve."

With a sudden lift of his head, he took in the living room, which was Maeve's finest creation. His eyes wandered from the bubblegum-pink cornice heading one wall, down the blue-and-silver-striped wallpaper, and landed on the purple velvet heart-backed chair. Beside it sat the yellow side table, which featured a bouquet of bright orange roses—silk—and a trio of tiny blue cats before the vase.

"What is this?"

He wandered into the room taking it all in as if he were in a gallery of strange and assorted oddities. Maeve felt an initial humiliation that he had discovered the very core of her, and then it fluttered off to be replaced by a satisfied nod. This was her home. She had created it. It was *her*. And if he didn't like it, then that sealed it: he could never like her. And she would have to accept that. Because she'd almost come to accept that they couldn't be a couple.

Almost.

"This." He stroked his fingers over the curve of a white and pink plaid lampshade. The violet fringe circling the bottom jiggled. "And this." A turn placed him before a bookshelf she'd painted lavender, which featured her and Lucy's book collection in color-coded order. "This is..."

He turned to her, his mouth open in awe. Did his eyes glint? Of course, they did. Those glacier blues were The Face's secret weapon. And she could smell his earthy violet color. Oh, how she'd missed that. Missed standing close to him. Missed the stroke of his fingers exploring her skin. His quiet summation of her. His deep laughter and playful manner. Missed everything about him.

"I know it offends your taste, Windfield," she offered, "but it's me."

"Yes, you and your ridiculous obsession with color." He studied the room a bit longer.

While she rubbed a hand up her arm. It wasn't ridiculous, it was who she was. Take her or leave her.

Just when she expected him to say something, he pulled her to him and kissed her.

Nothing could prepare her for the joy that melted across her skin and seeped into her veins. She'd been so worried she'd lost him. And now he was kissing her. Holding her against his body. Speaking to her with his lips, his tongue, his breath. She never wanted this to end. Could they stop time and exist without the world missing them?

"I've been thinking about your kiss for over

a week," he said. "Your dark cherry kisses. I dreamed about your riotous colors. They were the craziest and most exciting dreams I've ever had. And, well…" He gestured to take in the entire room. "This explains everything."

"Asher, I…"

He kissed her again. "I'm sorry. I realized that by rejecting Kichu as a client you took that as a rejection of you."

"You…you figured that out?"

"Yes, but in the moment, I was thinking that perhaps you had wanted me to fail—"

"I would never! Oh…" She winced when he met her gaze. "I mean, I may have considered that I could possibly represent Tony Kichu, but I knew it couldn't happen. And I genuinely wanted him as an artist for you. But I think I pushed too hard to get you to see beauty in something that was, truthfully, ugly."

"Kichu's artwork isn't for everyone, that's for certain. You really thought about representing him?"

She shrugged. "I have no experience. It was a wild dream."

"Dreams are supposed to be wild. Maeve, I don't want to push you out of my life. I love you."

Her mouth dropped open. Heartbeats thundered. And she couldn't stop herself from saying, "I do too. I love you. But…"

"But nothing. I'm learning, Maeve. It's a slow process, and I will get there."

"You're there. Trust me. You have my heart."

He placed a hand over her heart chakra, and she did the same to him. Then they laughed and kissed. "That woo-woo stuff is silly," he said. "We'll keep that our little secret."

"Trust me, I don't want anyone else touching your heart chakra."

"Same. But...I still believe I made the right call with Kichu. I could never be the best representative of his work. But I know who can be."

"Who? You didn't hand him over to Hammerstill?"

"Funny thing is, Kichu didn't want to work with that bombastic asshole either. He also made it clear he would never be comfortable working with me."

"You spoke to him again?"

Asher nodded. "I called him and stopped back into the resort yesterday on my way home. There was something I had to do. But first." He took his phone from his suit pocket and pressed the call button. "I've Krew and Joss waiting for a conference call. If you'll indulge me?"

Maeve shrugged. She wasn't sure what was going on. And she was still floating on his confession to being in love with her. Yes, oh, yes! Had she been thinking to apply for another job to put herself away from the only man she'd ever loved? Fool! His timing could not have been better. And yes, she truly believed this relationship had happened for a reason.

Krew answered and Joss called a hello. "You're at our Maeve's place?" Krew asked.

"Yes, well, er. Yes." Asher winked at her. "*My* Maeve is standing right here. I've told her that Kichu didn't want to work with either me or Hammerstill. I haven't told her who he does want to work with."

"Go ahead," Joss said. "Don't keep her in suspense."

"I don't understand," Maeve said. "What's the big secret?"

Holding the phone between them, Asher took her hand and said, "Tony Kichu asked if you would represent him as an artist for The Art Guys."

Maeve gaped. Her heartbeat doubled. This was incredible. But…

"Is she happy?" Krew asked.

"I'm not sure." Asher narrowed his gaze on her. "*Is* she happy?"

Maeve nodded. "Yes, but…I don't know what to say. It's very exciting. But can I do it? I mean, I've never represented an artist. And I'm only the receptionist."

"Maeve," Krew said, "we discussed this last

night. The three of us would like to promote you.
Rather, create a new position for you. Here's the
deal. We need you as the receptionist. You keep
our office and our lives in order. You are a wonder. But maybe you could be the receptionist
slash broker-in-training? We'd have you shadow
each of us in turn to learn the ropes. And eventually we'll replace you at the front desk. Of
course, your salary will increase. We don't want
to lose you, Maeve. Joss and I have been worried
since you returned from Iceland that something
was up. That you weren't happy here."

"Oh, I am. I mean…" There was still her dream
of someday opening her consulting shop. She had
to be honest with them. "Did Asher tell you guys
about my dream to open a shop?"

"I did." Asher took her hand. "They understand that you've a goal."

"And we're behind you one hundred percent,"
Joss said. "With the clout you'll gain working
with our network, that could transfer to you
gaining a bigger clientele."

That was all the encouragement she needed.
"Yes, I'd love to take on the new receptionist
slash broker-in-training position."

With a bounce she nodded to Asher, and he
thanked the guys and told them they'd stop in
tomorrow and the four of them could go over

Maeve's new role at The Art Guys. He hung up, and she plunged into his arms for a hug.

"You did that for me?"

"Honestly? It was Kichu's request. He felt the two of you bonded over his art. That you got him."

"I do get him."

"I understand that now that I stand here in your amazing home. This place, Maeve. It's a work of art."

"That drives you bonkers? Be honest."

"It's like I'm standing inside your brain. And I think Kichu created a great vision of it."

"Of what? My brain? I don't understand."

He picked up the wrapped canvas and handed it to her to unwrap. "I called him right after I arrived in Bangladesh. Asked him to create something that represented the two of us. I think he mastered it, yes?"

Maeve let the brown paper fall from the canvas and gasped at the sight of the colorful abstract. The black background held an explosion of colors, mainly greens, emeralds, blues and hints of the tangerine that she did adore. And yellow, her happy color! But there at the center was a dizzy spin of dusty violet. The very color she equated with Asher.

"Is that…" She pointed to the center.

"It's me. And you. Kichu said you were such

a riot of mystery and color that you could not be contained on the canvas. But that purple splotch in the middle is me, fitted into your heart. I asked him to do it like that. Do you like it? You'll be the first to own an official Kichu."

"Oh, Asher, it's perfect. This is incredible."

Setting aside the canvas, she spun and landed in his arms for a thankful hug. No pottery separating them this time. And no misunderstandings or faking. This was real.

"I love it here," he said. "With you. I can't imagine holding anyone else's hand. Hugging anyone else. Kissing anyone else. Maeve, you anchor me. I've been floating through life, getting by on a moniker that appeals in an aesthetic way, but those days I spent with you? I felt tethered. Grounded. You opened my eyes to discover the earthy and ugly."

"Yes, well, you didn't particularly care for the ugly."

"No, but I saw it. And I know it needs to be a part of my life to be fully whole. More rounded. Open. It's an amazing feeling. And I could think of but one thing this week I've been away. I want less The Face and more realness. Maeve, what I'm saying is that I'm in love with you and I want what started as a fake to be real."

She kissed him. "It is real. It really is."

EPILOGUE

SIX MONTHS LATER Maeve had introduced Tony Kichu's art to a select clientele. Maeve worked closely with Krew, who represented many clients who adored modern art, to match the perfect client to a specific canvas. But when the guys had suggested she add more artists to her list, she had politely declined. She was still finding her feet, accompanying Asher to auctions when he was in town and learning the ropes.

And honestly? She'd taken a new business plan for Fuchsia into The Art Guys and had shown it to the guys. Joss had already turned her on to one of his clients, who was looking for a colorful edit to her home.

"Do you think they're upset that I didn't want to take on more clients?" Maeve asked as Asher parked down the street from the rental space she'd been eyeing for Fuchsia.

"No, they knew this was your goal. Perhaps they're a little disappointed, because you're so good at what you do. They'll get over it. They know you're *our Maeve* and will always be a part of the family. But finding a new receptionist will be a challenge. You are irreplaceable."

"I'm not gone yet. And I do want to continue working with Kichu. I'm so glad you guys agreed to my suggestion for one day a week at the brokerage, and, well…it'll be a while before I switch to that schedule. I still need to qualify for a loan. That building is not cheap."

He turned off the car engine and leaned across to kiss her, then tipped up her chin. "I thought we'd discussed this?"

Asher had offered her a loan, zero percent interest. She would be a fool not to take it. They had been lovers for half a year. Boyfriend and girlfriend. Partners. They had kind of, sort of moved in together. After Lucy had left, Asher had offered to pick up the rent if he could use it as his landing place. An easy offer to accept. But still, he was only in the city four or five days a month. And yes, he did fly her in on the weekends to wherever in the world he was working. Two days of sightseeing, dining and lots of sex. And those three activities were not evenly divided. Maeve felt sure that visit to Morocco had been spent entirely in the room! Still, on the weekdays, she missed him desperately.

However, if she accepted money from him it would bind her to him in ways beyond the physical and even emotional. If anything did happen to their relationship it could become a sticking point that might destroy them both.

"You know I like to have control over my life," she said to his insistent stare.

"I do know that. But you also know when I say loan I mean a gift. Maeve, please let me do this for you? Let me give you a place where your dream can come alive in vivid color?"

She looked down the street where the shop sat. The Realtor had said he'd open it for an hour so she could stop in and make plans. It was the perfect place. And mentally, she had already painted the front in pink and violet stripes and the interior walls in pastel mint and peach and…

"Say yes?" Asher prompted.

Before logic could argue, she vigorously nodded. "Let's do this."

She rushed ahead to the shop and walked inside the dark room. The electricity had yet to be connected. Afternoon light beamed through the front plate glass window. The Realtor had left a flashlight across the room on a dusty counter that had once displayed handmade paper and ink pens.

The door jingled as Asher walked in, and she spun to find him going down on one knee before her. That charming smile caught her by surprise as he lifted a ring box before him.

"Maeve, the most strange yet beautiful color in my world. My favorite color. My heart chakra's soulmate. Would you marry me?"

Taken utterly by surprise, she clasped her hands against her chest. Her fantasy man had become her friend and lover. And now he wanted to be her husband? Overwhelmed and thrilled, she nodded as tears burst from her eyes.

Asher stood and slipped a beautiful ring on her finger. "The main stone is garnet," he said. "Because that is the color of you." He stroked her lips, then kissed her. "And the smaller stones circling it are amethyst."

"The color of you," she whispered. "Oh, Asher, I love you."

"Let's make a family together. Beautiful and lush and earthy and even a little ugly." He laughed, and she bowed her head to his. "To a colorful future."

* * * * *